OBSCURE DESTINIES

WILLA CATHER

OBSCURE DESTINIES

VINTAGE BOOKS
A Division of Random House · New York

VINTAGE BOOKS EDITION,
September 1974

Library of Congress Cataloging in Publication Data

Cather, Willa Sibert, 1873–1947.
Obscure destinies.
CONTENTS: Neighbour Rosicky.—Old Mrs. Harris.—
Two friends.
I. Title.
PZ3.C28580f9   [PS3505.A87]   813'.5'2   74–5324
ISBN 0-394-71179-3

CONTENTS

NEIGHBOUR ROSICKY

NEIGHBOUR ROSICKY

I

When Doctor Burleigh told neighbour Rosicky he had a bad heart, Rosicky protested.

"So? No, I guess my heart was always pretty good. I got a little asthma, maybe. Just a awful short breath when I was pitchin' hay last summer, dat's all."

"Well now, Rosicky, if you know more about it than I do, what did you come to me for? It's your heart that makes you short of breath, I tell you. You're sixty-five years old, and you've always worked hard, and your heart's tired. You've got to be careful from now on, and you can't do heavy work any more. You've got five boys at home to do it for you."

The old farmer looked up at the Doctor with a gleam of amusement in his queer triangular-shaped eyes. His eyes were large and lively, but the lids were caught up in the middle in a curious way, so that they formed a triangle. He did not look like a sick man. His brown face was creased but not wrinkled, he had a ruddy colour in his smooth-shaven cheeks and in his lips, under his long brown moustache. His hair was thin and ragged around his ears, but very little grey. His forehead, naturally high and crossed by deep parallel lines, now ran all the way up to his pointed crown. Rosicky's face had the habit of looking interested, — suggested a contented disposition and a reflective quality that was gay rather than grave. This gave him a certain detachment, the easy manner of an onlooker and observer.

"Well, I guess you ain't got no pills fur a bad heart, Doctor Ed. I guess the only thing is fur me to git me a new one."

Doctor Burleigh swung round in his desk-chair and frowned at the old farmer. "I think if I were you I'd take a little care of the old one, Rosicky."

Rosicky shrugged. "Maybe I don't know how. I expect you mean fur me not to drink my coffee no more."

"I wouldn't, in your place. But you'll do as you choose about that. I've never yet been able to separate a Bohemian from his coffee or his pipe. I've quit trying. But the sure thing is you've got to cut out farm work. You can feed the stock and do chores about the barn, but you can't do anything in the fields that makes you short of breath."

"How about shelling corn?"

"Of course not!"

Rosicky considered with puckered brows.

"I can't make my heart go no longer'n it wants to, can I, Doctor Ed?"

"I think it's good for five or six years yet, maybe more, if you'll take the strain off it. Sit around the house and help Mary. If I had a good wife like yours, I'd want to stay around the house."

His patient chuckled. "It ain't no place fur a man. I don't like no old man hanging round the kitchen too much. An' my wife, she's a awful hard worker her own self."

"That's it; you can help her a little. My Lord, Rosicky, you are one of the few men I know who has a family he can get some comfort out of; happy dispositions, never quarrel among themselves, and they treat you right. I want to see you live a few years and enjoy them."

"Oh, they're good kids, all right," Rosicky assented.

The Doctor wrote him a prescription and asked him how his oldest son, Rudolph, who had married in the spring, was getting on.

Rudolph had struck out for himself, on rented land. " And how's Polly? I was afraid Mary mightn't like an American daughter-in-law, but it seems to be working out all right."

" Yes, she's a fine girl. Dat widder woman bring her daughters up very nice. Polly got lots of spunk, an' she got some style, too. Da's nice, for young folks to have some style." Rosicky inclined his head gallantly. His voice and his twinkly smile were an affectionate compliment to his daughter-in-law.

" It looks like a storm, and you'd better be getting home before it comes. In town in the car? " Doctor Burleigh rose.

" No, I'm in de wagon. When you got five boys, you ain't got much chance to ride round in de Ford. I ain't much for cars, noway."

" Well, it's a good road out to your place; but I don't want you bumping around in a wagon much. And never again on a hay-rake, remember! "

Rosicky placed the Doctor's fee delicately behind the desk-telephone, looking the other way, as if this were an absent-minded gesture.

He put on his plush cap and his corduroy jacket with a sheepskin collar, and went out.

The Doctor picked up his stethoscope and frowned at it as if he were seriously annoyed with the instrument. He wished it had been telling tales about some other man's heart, some old man who didn't look the Doctor in the eye so knowingly, or hold out such a warm brown hand when he said good-bye. Doctor Burleigh had been a poor boy in the country before he went away to medical school; he had known Rosicky almost ever since he could remember, and he had a deep affection for Mrs. Rosicky.

Only last winter he had had such a good breakfast at Rosicky's, and that when he needed it. He had been out all night on a long, hard confinement case at Tom Marshall's, — a big rich farm where there was plenty of stock and plenty of feed and a great deal of expensive farm machinery of the newest model, and no comfort whatever. The woman had too many children and too much work, and she was no manager. When the baby was born at last, and handed over to the assisting neighbour woman, and the mother was properly attended to, Burleigh refused any breakfast in that slovenly house, and drove his buggy — the snow was too deep for a car — eight miles to Anton Rosicky's place. He didn't know another farm-house where a man could get such a warm welcome, and such good strong coffee with rich cream. No wonder the old chap didn't want to give up his coffee!

He had driven in just when the boys had come back from the barn and were washing up for breakfast. The long table, covered with a bright oilcloth, was set out with dishes waiting for them, and the warm kitchen was full of the smell of coffee and hot biscuit and sausage. Five big handsome boys, running from twenty to twelve, all with what Burleigh called natural good manners, — they hadn't a bit of the painful self-consciousness he himself had to struggle with when he was a lad. One ran to put his horse away, another helped him off with his fur coat and hung it up, and Josephine, the youngest child and the only daughter, quickly set another place under her mother's direction.

With Mary, to feed creatures was the natural expression of affection, — her chickens, the calves, her big hungry boys. It was a rare pleasure to feed a young man whom she seldom saw and of whom she was as proud as if he belonged to her. Some country housekeepers would have stopped to spread a white cloth over the oilcloth, to change the thick cups and plates for their best china, and the wooden-handled knives for plated ones. But not Mary.

" You must take us as you find us, Doctor Ed. I'd be glad to put out my good things for you if you was expected, but I'm glad to get you any way at all."

He knew she was glad, — she threw back her head and spoke out as if she were announcing him to the whole prairie. Rosicky hadn't said anything at all; he merely smiled his twinkling smile, put some more coal on the fire, and went into his own room to pour the Doctor a little drink in a medicine glass. When they were all seated, he watched his wife's face from his end of the table and spoke to her in Czech. Then, with the instinct of politeness which seldom failed him, he turned to the Doctor and said slyly; " I was just tellin' her not to ask you no questions about Mrs. Marshall till you eat some breakfast. My wife, she's terrible fur to ask questions."

The boys laughed, and so did Mary. She watched the Doctor devour her biscuit and sausage, too much excited to eat anything herself. She drank her coffee and sat taking in everything about her visitor. She had known him when he was a poor country boy, and was boastfully proud of his success, always saying: " What do people go to Omaha for, to see a doctor, when we got the best one in the State right here? " If Mary liked people at all, she felt physical pleasure in the sight of them, personal exultation in any good fortune that came to them. Burleigh didn't know many women like that, but he knew she was like that.

When his hunger was satisfied, he did, of course, have to tell them about Mrs. Marshall, and he noticed what a friendly interest the boys took in the matter.

Rudolph, the oldest one (he was still living at home then), said: " The last time I was over there, she was lifting them big heavy milk-cans, and I knew she oughtn't to be doing it."

" Yes, Rudolph told me about that when he come home, and I said it wasn't right," Mary put in warmly. " It was all right for me to do them things up to the last, for I was terrible strong, but that woman's weakly. And do you think she'll be able to nurse it, Ed? " She sometimes forgot to give him the title she was so proud of. " And to think of your being up all night and then not able to get a decent breakfast! I don't know what's the matter with such people."

" Why, Mother," said one of the boys, " if Doctor Ed had got breakfast there, we wouldn't have him here. So you ought to be glad."

" He knows I'm glad to have him, John, any time. But I'm sorry for that poor woman, how bad she'll feel the Doctor had to go away in the cold without his breakfast."

"I wish I'd been in practice when these were getting born." The doctor looked down the row of close-clipped heads. "I missed some good breakfasts by not being."

The boys began to laugh at their mother because she flushed so red, but she stood her ground and threw up her head. "I don't care, you wouldn't have got away from this house without breakfast. No doctor ever did. I'd have had something ready fixed that Anton could warm up for you."

The boys laughed harder than ever, and exclaimed at her: "I'll bet you would!" "She would, that!"

"Father, did you get breakfast for the doctor when we were born?"

"Yes, and he used to bring me my breakfast, too, mighty nice. I was always awful hungry!" Mary admitted with a guilty laugh.

While the boys were getting the Doctor's horse, he went to the window to examine the house plants. "What do you do to your geraniums to keep them blooming all winter, Mary? I never pass this house that from the road I don't see your windows full of flowers."

She snapped off a dark red one, and a ruffled new green leaf, and put them in his buttonhole. " There, that looks better. You look too solemn for a young man, Ed. Why don't you git married? I'm worried about you. Settin' at breakfast, I looked at you real hard, and I seen you've got some grey hairs already."

" Oh, yes! They're coming. Maybe they'd come faster if I married."

"Don't talk so. You'll ruin your health eating at the hotel. I could send your wife a nice loaf of nut bread, if you only had one. I don't like to see a young man getting grey. I'll tell you something, Ed; you make some strong black tea and keep it handy in a bowl, and every morning just brush it into your hair, an' it'll keep the grey from showin' much. That's the way I do! "

Sometimes the Doctor heard the gossipers in the drug-store wondering why Rosicky didn't get on faster. He was industrious, and so were his boys, but they were rather free and easy, weren't pushers, and they didn't always show good judgment. They were comfortable, they were out of debt, but they didn't get much ahead. Maybe, Doctor Burleigh reflected, people as generous and warm-hearted and affectionate as the Rosickys never got ahead much; maybe you couldn't enjoy your life and put it into the bank, too.

II

When Rosicky left Doctor Burleigh's office he went into the farm-implement store to light his pipe and put on his glasses and read over the list Mary had given him. Then he went into the general merchandise place next door and stood about until the pretty girl with the plucked eyebrows, who always waited on him, was free. Those eyebrows, two thin India-ink strokes, amused him, because he remembered how they used to be. Rosicky always prolonged his shopping by a little joking; the girl knew the old fellow admired her, and she liked to chaff with him.

"Seems to me about every other week you buy ticking, Mr. Rosicky, and always the best quality," she remarked as she measured off the heavy bolt with red stripes.

"You see, my wife is always makin' goose-fedder pillows, an' de thin stuff don't hold in dem little down-fedders."

"You must have lots of pillows at your house."

"Sure. She makes quilts of dem, too. We sleeps easy. Now she's makin' a fedder quilt for my son's wife. You know Polly, that married my Rudolph. How much my bill, Miss Pearl?"

"Eight eighty-five."

"Chust make it nine, and put in some candy fur de women."

"As usual. I never did see a man buy so much candy for his wife. First thing you know, she'll be getting too fat."

"I'd like dat. I ain't much fur all dem slim women like what de style is now."

"That's one for me, I suppose, Mr. Bo-hunk!" Pearl sniffed and elevated her India-ink strokes.

When Rosicky went out to his wagon, it was beginning to snow, — the first snow of the season, and he was glad to see it. He rattled out of town and along the highway through a wonderfully rich stretch of country, the finest farms in the county. He admired this High Prairie, as it was called, and always liked to drive through it. His own place lay in a rougher territory, where there was some clay in the soil and it was not so productive. When he bought his land, he hadn't the money to buy on High Prairie; so he told his boys, when they grumbled, that if their land hadn't some clay in it, they wouldn't own it at all. All the same, he enjoyed looking at these fine farms, as he enjoyed looking at a prize bull.

After he had gone eight miles, he came to the graveyard, which lay just at the edge of his own hay-land. There he stopped his horses and sat still on his wagon seat, looking about at the snowfall. Over yonder on the hill he could see his own house, crouching low, with the clump of orchard behind and the windmill before, and all down the gentle hill-slope the rows of pale gold cornstalks stood out against the white field. The snow was falling over the cornfield and the pasture and the hay-land, steadily, with very little wind, — a nice dry snow. The grave-yard had only a light wire fence about it and was all overgrown with long red grass. The fine snow, settling into this red grass and upon the few little evergreens and the headstones, looked very pretty.

It was a nice graveyard, Rosicky reflected, sort of snug and homelike, not cramped or mournful, — a big sweep all round it. A man could lie down in the long grass and see the complete arch of the sky over him, hear the wagons go by; in summer the mowing-machine rattled right up to the wire fence. And it was so near home. Over there across the cornstalks his own roof and windmill looked so good to him that he promised himself to mind the Doc-tor and take care of himself. He was awful fond of his place, he admitted. He wasn't anxious to leave it. And it was a comfort to think that he would never have to go farther than the edge of his own hayfield. The snow, falling over his barnyard and the graveyard, seemed to draw things together like. And they were all old neighbours in the graveyard, most of them friends; there was nothing to feel awkward or embarrassed about. Embarrassment was the most disagreeable feeling Rosicky knew. He didn't often have it, — only with certain people whom he didn't understand at all.

Well, it was a nice snowstorm; a fine sight to see the snow falling so quietly and graciously over so much open country. On his cap and shoulders, on the horses' backs and manes, light, delicate, mysterious it fell; and with it a dry cool fragrance was released into the air. It meant rest for vegetation and men and beasts, for the ground itself; a season of long nights for sleep, leisurely breakfasts, peace by the fire. This and much more went through Rosicky's mind, but he merely told himself that winter was coming, clucked to his horses, and drove on.

When he reached home, John, the youngest boy, ran out to put away his team for him, and he met Mary coming up from the outside cellar with her apron full of carrots. They went into the house together. On the table, covered with oilcloth figured with clusters of blue grapes, a place was set, and he smelled hot coffee-cake of some kind. Anton never lunched in town; he thought that extravagant, and anyhow he didn't like the food. So Mary always had something ready for him when he got home.

After he was settled in his chair, stirring his coffee in a big cup, Mary took out of the oven a pan of *kolache* stuffed with apricots, examined them anxiously to see whether they had got too dry, put them beside his plate, and then sat down opposite him.

Rosicky asked her in Czech if she wasn't going to have any coffee.

She replied in English, as being somehow the right language for transacting business: "Now what did Doctor Ed say, Anton? You tell me just what."

"He said I was to tell you some compliments, but I forgot 'em." Rosicky's eyes twinkled.

"About you, I mean. What did he say about your asthma?"

"He says I ain't got no asthma." Rosicky took one of the little rolls in his broad brown fingers. The thickened nail of his right thumb told the story of his past.

"Well, what is the matter? And don't try to put me off."

"He don't say nothing much, only I'm a little older, and my heart ain't so good like it used to be."

Mary started and brushed her hair back from her temples with both hands as if she were a little out of her mind. From the way she glared, she might have been in a rage with him.

"He says there's something the matter with your heart? Doctor Ed says so?"

"Now don't yell at me like I was a hog in de garden, Mary. You know I always did like to hear a woman talk soft. He didn't say anything de matter wid my heart, only it ain't so young like it used to be, an' he tell me not to pitch hay or run de corn-sheller."

Mary wanted to jump up, but she sat still. She admired the way he never under any circumstances raised his voice or spoke roughly. He was city-bred, and she was country-bred; she often said she wanted her boys to have their papa's nice ways.

"You never have no pain there, do you? It's your breathing and your stomach that's been wrong. I wouldn't believe nobody but Doctor Ed about it. I guess I'll go see him myself. Didn't he give you no advice?"

"Chust to take it easy like, an' stay round de house dis winter. I guess you got some carpenter work for me to do. I kin make some new shelves for you, and I want dis long time to build a closet in de boys' room and make dem two little fellers keep dere clo'es hung up."

Rosicky drank his coffee from time to time, while he considered. His moustache was of the soft long variety and came down over his mouth like the teeth of a buggy-rake over a bundle of hay. Each time he put down his cup,

he ran his blue handkerchief over his lips.
When he took a drink of water, he managed
very neatly with the back of his hand.

Mary sat watching him intently, trying to
find any change in his face. It is hard to see anyone who has become like your own body to you.
Yes, his hair had got thin, and his high forehead
had deep lines running from left to right. But
his neck, always clean shaved except in the busi-
est seasons, was not loose or baggy. It was
burned a dark reddish brown, and there were
deep creases in it, but it looked firm and full of
blood. His cheeks had a good colour. On either
side of his mouth there was a half-moon down
the length of his cheek, not wrinkles, but two
lines that had come there from his habitual expression. He was shorter and broader than
when she married him; his back had grown
broad and curved, a good deal like the shell of
an old turtle, and his arms and legs were short.

He was fifteen years older than Mary, but
she had hardly ever thought about it before. He
was her man, and the kind of man she liked.
She was rough, and he was gentle, — city-bred,

as she always said. They had been shipmates on a rough voyage and had stood by each other in trying times. Life had gone well with them because, at bottom, they had the same ideas about life. They agreed, without discussion, as to what was most important and what was secondary. They didn't often exchange opinions, even in Czech, — it was as if they had thought the same thought together. A good deal had to be sacrificed and thrown overboard in a hard life like theirs, and they had never disagreed as to the things that could go. It had been a hard life, and a soft life, too. There wasn't anything brutal in the short, broad-backed man with the three-cornered eyes and the forehead that went on to the top of his skull. He was a city man, a gentle man, and though he had married a rough farm girl, he had never touched her without gentleness.

They had been at one accord not to hurry through life, not to be always skimping and saving. They saw their neighbours buy more land and feed more stock than they did, without discontent. Once when the creamery agent came to the Rosickys to persuade them to sell him their cream, he told them how much money the Fasslers, their nearest neighbours, had made on their cream last year.

" Yes," said Mary, " and look at them Fassler children! Pale, pinched little things, they look like skimmed milk. I'd rather put some colour into my children's faces than put money into the bank."

The agent shrugged and turned to Anton.

" I guess we'll do like she says," said Rosicky.

III

Mary very soon got into town to see Doctor Ed, and then she had a talk with her boys and set a guard over Rosicky. Even John, the youngest, had his father on his mind. If Rosicky went to throw hay down from the loft, one of the boys ran up the ladder and took the fork from him. He sometimes complained that though he was getting to be an old man, he wasn't an old woman yet.

That winter he stayed in the house in the afternoons and carpentered, or sat in the chair between the window full of plants and the wooden bench where the two pails of drinking-water stood. This spot was called "Father's corner," though it was not a corner at all. He had a shelf there, where he kept his Bohemian papers and his pipes and tobacco, and his shears and needles and thread and tailor's thimble. Having been a tailor in his youth, he couldn't bear to see a woman patching at his clothes, or at the boys'. He liked tailoring, and always patched all the overalls and jackets and work shirts. Occasionally he made over a pair of pants one of the older boys had outgrown, for the little fellow.

While he sewed, he let his mind run back over his life. He had a good deal to remember, really; life in three countries. The only part of his youth he didn't like to remember was the two years he had spent in London, in Cheapside, working for a German tailor who was wretchedly poor. Those days, when he was nearly always hungry, when his clothes were dropping off him for dirt, and the sound of a strange language kept him in continual bewilderment, had left a sore spot in his mind that wouldn't bear touching.

He was twenty when he landed at Castle Garden in New York, and he had a protector who got him work in a tailor shop in Vesey Street, down near the Washington Market. He looked upon that part of his life as very happy. He became a good workman, he was industrious, and his wages were increased from time to time. He minded his own business and envied nobody's good fortune. He went to night school and learned to read English. He often did overtime work and was well paid for it, but somehow he never saved anything. He couldn't refuse a loan to a friend, and he was self-indulgent. He liked a good dinner, and a little went for beer, a little for tobacco; a good deal went to the girls. He often stood through an opera on Saturday nights; he could get standing-room for a dollar. Those were the great days of opera in New York, and it gave a fellow something to think about for the rest of the week. Rosicky had a quick ear, and a childish love of all the stage splendour; the scenery, the costumes, the ballet. He usually went with a chum, and after the performance they had beer and maybe some oysters somewhere. It was a fine life; for the first five years or so it satisfied him completely. He was never hungry or cold or dirty, and everything amused him: a fire, a dog fight, a parade, a storm, a ferry ride. He thought New York the finest, richest, friendliest city in the world.

Moreover, he had what he called a happy home life. Very near the tailor shop was a small furniture-factory, where an old Austrian, Loeffler, employed a few skilled men and made unusual furniture, most of it to order, for the rich German housewives up-town. The top floor of Loeffler's five-storey factory was a loft, where he kept his choice lumber and stored the odd pieces of furniture left on his hands. One of the young workmen he employed was a Czech, and he and Rosicky became fast friends. They persuaded Loeffler to let them have a sleeping-room in one corner of the loft. They bought good beds and bedding and had their pick of the furniture kept up there. The loft was low-pitched, but light and airy, full of windows, and good-smelling by reason of the fine lumber put up there to season. Old Loeffler used to go down to the docks and buy wood from South America and the East from the sea captains. The young men were as foolish about their house as a bridal pair. Zichec, the young cabinet-maker, devised every sort of convenience, and Rosicky kept their clothes in order. At night and on Sundays, when the quiver of machinery underneath was still, it was the quietest place in the world, and on summer nights all the sea winds blew in. Zichec often practised on his flute in the evening. They were both fond of music and went to the opera together. Rosicky thought he wanted to live like that for ever.

But as the years passed, all alike, he began to get a little restless. When spring came round, he would begin to feel fretted, and he got to drinking. He was likely to drink too much of a Saturday night. On Sunday he was languid and heavy, getting over his spree. On Monday he plunged into work again. So he never had time to figure out what ailed him, though he knew something did. When the grass turned green in Park Place, and the lilac hedge at the back of Trinity churchyard put out its blossoms, he was tormented by a longing to run away. That was why he drank too much; to get a temporary illusion of freedom and wide horizons.

Rosicky, the old Rosicky, could remember as if it were yesterday the day when the young Rosicky found out what was the matter with him. It was on a Fourth of July afternoon, and he was sitting in Park Place in the sun. The lower part of New York was empty. Wall Street, Liberty Street, Broadway, all empty. So much stone and asphalt with nothing going on, so many empty windows. The emptiness was intense, like the stillness in a great factory when the machinery stops and the belts and bands cease running. It was too great a change, it took all the strength out of one. Those blank buildings, without the stream of life pouring through them, were like empty jails. It struck young Rosicky that this was the trouble with big cities; they built you in from the earth itself, cemented you away from any contact with the ground. You lived in an unnatural world, like the fish in an aquarium, who were probably much more comfortable than they ever were in the sea.

On that very day he began to think seriously about the articles he had read in the Bohemian papers, describing prosperous Czech farming communities in the West. He believed he would like to go out there as a farm hand; it was hardly possible that he could ever have land of his own. His people had always been workmen; his father and grandfather had worked in shops. His mother's parents had lived in the country, but they rented their farm and had a hard time to get along. Nobody in his family had ever owned any land, — that belonged to a different station of life altogether. Anton's mother died when he was little, and he was sent into the country to her parents. He stayed with them until he was twelve, and formed those ties with the earth and the farm animals and growing things which are never made at all unless they are made early. After his grandfather died, he went back to live with his father and stepmother, but she was very hard on him, and his father helped him to get passage to London.

After that Fourth of July day in Park Place, the desire to return to the country never left him. To work on another man's farm would be all he asked; to see the sun rise and set and to plant things and watch them grow. He was a very simple man. He was like a tree that has not many roots, but one tap-root that goes down deep. He subscribed for a Bohemian paper printed in Chicago, then for one printed in Omaha. His mind got farther and farther west. He began to save a little money to buy his liberty. When he was thirty-five, there was a great meeting in New York of Bohemian athletic societies, and Rosicky left the tailor shop and went home with the Omaha delegates to try his fortune in another part of the world.

IV

Perhaps the fact that his own youth was well over before he began to have a family was one reason why Rosicky was so fond of his boys. He had almost a grandfather's indulgence for them. He had never had to worry about any of them — except, just now, a little about Rudolph.

On Saturday night the boys always piled into the Ford, took little Josephine, and went to town to the moving-picture show. One Saturday morning they were talking at the breakfast table about starting early that evening, so that they would have an hour or so to see the Christmas things in the stores before the show began. Rosicky looked down the table.

"I hope you boys ain't disappointed, but I want you to let me have de car tonight. Maybe some of you can go in with de neighbours."

Their faces fell. They worked hard all week, and they were still like children. A new jack-knife or a box of candy pleased the older ones as much as the little fellow.

"If you and Mother are going to town," Frank said, "maybe you could take a couple of us along with you, anyway."

"No, I want to take de car down to Rudolph's, and let him an' Polly go in to de show. She don't git into town enough, an' I'm afraid she's gettin' lonesome, an' he can't afford no car yet."

That settled it. The boys were a good deal dashed. Their father took another piece of apple-cake and went on: "Maybe next Saturday night de two little fellers can go along wid dem."

"Oh, is Rudolph going to have the car every Saturday night?"

Rosicky did not reply at once; then he began to speak seriously: "Listen, boys; Polly ain't lookin' so good. I don't like to see nobody lookin' sad. It comes hard fur a town girl to be a farmer's wife. I don't want no trouble to start in Rudolph's family. When it starts, it ain't so easy to stop. An American girl don't git used to our ways all at once. I like to tell Polly she and Rudolph can have the car every Saturday night till after New Year's, if it's all right with you boys."

"Sure it's all right, Papa," Mary cut in. "And it's good you thought about that. Town girls is used to more than country girls. I lay awake nights, scared she'll make Rudolph discontented with the farm."

The boys put as good a face on it as they could. They surely looked forward to their Saturday nights in town. That evening Rosicky drove the car the half-mile down to Rudolph's new, bare little house.

Polly was in a short-sleeved gingham dress, clearing away the supper dishes. She was a trim, slim little thing, with blue eyes and shingled yellow hair, and her eyebrows were reduced to a mere brush-stroke, like Miss Pearl's.

"Good evening, Mr. Rosicky. Rudolph's at the barn, I guess." She never called him father, or Mary mother. She was sensitive about having married a foreigner. She never in the world would have done it if Rudolph hadn't been such a handsome, persuasive fellow and such a gallant lover. He had graduated in her class in the high school in town, and their friendship began in the ninth grade.

Rosicky went in, though he wasn't exactly asked. " My boys ain't goin' to town tonight, an' I brought de car over fur you two to go in to de picture show."

Polly, carrying dishes to the sink, looked over her shoulder at him. " Thank you. But I'm late with my work tonight, and pretty tired. Maybe Rudolph would like to go in with you."

" Oh, I don't go to de shows! I'm too old-fashioned. You won't feel so tired after you ride in de air a ways. It's a nice clear night, an' it ain't cold. You go an' fix yourself up, Polly, an' I'll wash de dishes an' leave everything nice fur you."

Polly blushed and tossed her bob. " I couldn't let you do that, Mr. Rosicky. I wouldn't think of it."

Rosicky said nothing. He found a bib apron on a nail behind the kitchen door. He slipped it over his head and then took Polly by her two elbows and pushed her gently toward the door of her own room. "I washed up de kitchen many times for my wife, when de babies was sick or somethin'. You go an' make yourself look nice. I like you to look prettier'n any of dem town girls when you go in. De young folks must have some fun, an' I'm goin' to look out fur you, Polly."

That kind, reassuring grip on her elbows, the old man's funny bright eyes, made Polly want to drop her head on his shoulder for a second. She restrained herself, but she lingered in his grasp at the door of her room, murmuring tearfully: "You always lived in the city when you were young, didn't you? Don't you ever get lonesome out here?"

As she turned round to him, her hand fell naturally into his, and he stood holding it and smiling into her face with his peculiar, knowing, indulgent smile without a shadow of reproach in it. "Dem big cities is all right fur de rich, but dey is terrible hard fur de poor."

"I don't know. Sometimes I think I'd like to take a chance. You lived in New York, didn't you?"

" An' London. Da's bigger still. I learned my trade dere. Here's Rudolph comin', you better hurry."

" Will you tell me about London some time? "

" Maybe. Only I ain't no talker, Polly. Run an' dress yourself up."

The bedroom door closed behind her, and Rudolph came in from the outside, looking anxious. He had seen the car and was sorry any of his family should come just then. Supper hadn't been a very pleasant occasion. Halting in the doorway, he saw his father in a kitchen apron, carrying dishes to the sink. He flushed crimson and something flashed in his eye. Rosicky held up a warning finger.

" I brought de car over fur you an' Polly to go to de picture show, an' I made her let me finish here so you won't be late. You go put on a clean shirt, quick! "

" But don't the boys want the car, Father? "

" Not tonight dey don't." Rosicky fumbled under his apron and found his pants pocket. He took out a silver dollar and said in a hurried whisper: " You go an' buy dat girl some ice cream an' candy tonight, like you was courtin'. She's awful good friends wid me."

Rudolph was very short of cash, but he took the money as if it hurt him. There had been a crop failure all over the county. He had more than once been sorry he'd married this year.

In a few minutes the young people came out, looking clean and a little stiff. Rosicky hurried them off, and then he took his own time with the dishes. He scoured the pots and pans and put away the milk and swept the kitchen. He put some coal in the stove and shut off the draughts, so the place would be warm for them when they got home late at night. Then he sat down and had a pipe and listened to the clock tick.

Generally speaking, marrying an American girl was certainly a risk. A Czech should marry a Czech. It was lucky that Polly was the daughter of a poor widow woman; Rudolph was proud, and if she had a prosperous family to throw up at him, they could never make it go. Polly was one of four sisters, and they all worked; one was book-keeper in the bank, one taught music, and Polly and her younger sister had been clerks, like Miss Pearl. All four of them were musical, had pretty voices, and sang in the Methodist choir, which the eldest sister directed.

Polly missed the sociability of a store position. She missed the choir, and the company of her sisters. She didn't dislike housework, but she disliked so much of it. Rosicky was a little anxious about this pair. He was afraid Polly would grow so discontented that Rudy would quit the farm and take a factory job in Omaha. He had worked for a winter up there, two years ago, to get money to marry on. He had done very well, and they would always take him back at the stockyards. But to Rosicky that meant the end of everything for his son. To be a landless man was to be a wage-earner, a slave, all your life; to have nothing, to be nothing.

Rosicky thought he would come over and do a little carpentering for Polly after the New Year. He guessed she needed jollying. Rudolph was a serious sort of chap, serious in love and serious about his work.

Rosicky shook out his pipe and walked home across the fields. Ahead of him the lamplight shone from his kitchen windows. Suppose he were still in a tailor shop on Vesey Street, with a bunch of pale, narrow-chested sons working on machines, all coming home tired and sullen to eat supper in a kitchen that was a parlour also; with another crowded, angry family quarrelling just across the dumb-waiter shaft, and squeaking pulleys at the windows where dirty washings hung on dirty lines above a court full of old brooms and mops and ash-cans. . . .

He stopped by the windmill to look up at the frosty winter stars and draw a long breath before he went inside. That kitchen with the shining windows was dear to him; but the sleeping fields and bright stars and the noble darkness were dearer still.

V

On the day before Christmas the weather set in very cold; no snow, but a bitter, biting wind that whistled and sang over the flat land and lashed one's face like fine wires. There was baking going on in the Rosicky kitchen all day, and Rosicky sat inside, making over a coat that Albert had outgrown into an overcoat for John. Mary had a big red geranium in bloom for Christmas, and a row of Jerusalem cherry trees, full of berries. It was the first year she had ever grown these; Doctor Ed brought her the seeds from Omaha when he went to some medical convention. They reminded Rosicky of plants he had seen in England; and all afternoon, as he stitched, he sat thinking about those two years in London, which his mind usually shrank from even after all this while.

He was a lad of eighteen when he dropped down into London, with no money and no connexions except the address of a cousin who was supposed to be working at a confectioner's. When he went to the pastry shop, however, he

found that the cousin had gone to America.
Anton tramped the streets for several days,
sleeping in doorways and on the Embankment,
until he was in utter despair. He knew no English, and the sound of the strange language all
about him confused him. By chance he met a
poor German tailor who had learned his trade
in Vienna, and could speak a little Czech. This
tailor, Lifschnitz, kept a repair shop in a
Cheapside basement, underneath a cobbler.
He didn't much need an apprentice, but he
was sorry for the boy and took him in for no
wages but his keep and what he could pick up.
The pickings were supposed to be coppers
given you when you took work home to a customer. But most of the customers called for
their clothes themselves, and the coppers that
came Anton's way were very few. He had,
however, a place to sleep. The tailor's family
lived upstairs in three rooms; a kitchen, a bedroom, where Lifschnitz and his wife and five
children slept, and a living-room. Two corners
of this living-room were curtained off for lodg-
ers; in one Rosicky slept on an old horsehair

sofa, with a feather quilt to wrap himself in.
The other corner was rented to a wretched,
dirty boy, who was studying the violin. He
actually practised there. Rosicky was dirty,
too. There was no way to be anything else.
Mrs. Lifschnitz got the water she cooked and
washed with from a pump in a brick court,
four flights down. There were bugs in the
place, and multitudes of fleas, though the poor
woman did the best she could. Rosicky knew
she often went empty to give another potato
or a spoonful of dripping to the two hungry,
sad-eyed boys who lodged with her. He used
to think he would never get out of there, never
get a clean shirt to his back again. What would
he do, he wondered, when his clothes actually
dropped to pieces and the worn cloth wouldn't
hold patches any longer?

It was still early when the old farmer put
aside his sewing and his recollections. The sky
had been a dark grey all day, with not a gleam
of sun, and the light failed at four o'clock. He
went to shave and change his shirt while the

turkey was roasting. Rudolph and Polly were coming over for supper.

After supper they sat round in the kitchen, and the younger boys were saying how sorry they were it hadn't snowed. Everybody was sorry. They wanted a deep snow that would lie long and keep the wheat warm, and leave the ground soaked when it melted.

"Yes, sir!" Rudolph broke out fiercely; "if we have another dry year like last year, there's going to be hard times in this country."

Rosicky filled his pipe. "You boys don't know what hard times is. You don't owe nobody, you got plenty to eat an' keep warm, an' plenty water to keep clean. When you got them, you can't have it very hard."

Rudolph frowned, opened and shut his big right hand, and dropped it clenched upon his knee. "I've got to have a good deal more than that, Father, or I'll quit this farming gamble. I can always make good wages railroading, or at the packing house, and be sure of my money."

"Maybe so," his father answered dryly.

Mary, who had just come in from the pantry and was wiping her hands on the roller towel, thought Rudy and his father were getting too serious. She brought her darning-basket and sat down in the middle of the group.

"I ain't much afraid of hard times, Rudy," she said heartily. "We've had a plenty, but we've always come through. Your father wouldn't never take nothing very hard, not even hard times. I got a mind to tell you a story on him. Maybe you boys can't hardly remember the year we had that terrible hot wind, that burned everything up on the Fourth of July? All the corn an' the gardens. An' that was in the days when we didn't have alfalfa yet, — I guess it wasn't invented.

"Well, that very day your father was out cultivatin' corn, and I was here in the kitchen makin' plum preserves. We had bushels of plums that year. I noticed it was terrible hot, but it's always hot in the kitchen when you're preservin', an' I was too busy with my plums to mind. Anton come in from the field about three o'clock, an' I asked him what was the matter.

"'Nothin',' he says, 'but it's pretty hot, an' I think I won't work no more today.' He stood round for a few minutes, an' then he says: 'Ain't you near through? I want you should git up a nice supper for us tonight. It's Fourth of July.'

"I told him to git along, that I was right in the middle of preservin', but the plums would taste good on hot biscuit. 'I'm goin' to have fried chicken, too,' he says, and he went off an' killed a couple. You three oldest boys was little fellers, playin' round outside, real hot an' sweaty, an' your father took you to the horse tank down by the windmill an' took off your clothes an' put you in. Them two box-elder trees was little then, but they made shade over the tank. Then he took off all his own clothes, an' got in with you. While he was playin' in the water with you, the Methodist preacher drove into our place to say how all the neighbours was goin' to meet at the schoolhouse that night, to pray for rain. He drove right to the windmill, of course, and there was your father and you three with no clothes on. I was in the kitchen door, an' I had to laugh, for the preacher acted like he ain't never seen a naked man before. He surely was embarrassed, an' your father couldn't git to his clothes; they was all hangin' up on the windmill to let the sweat dry out of 'em. So he laid in the tank where he was, an' put one of you boys on top of him to cover him up a little, an' talked to the preacher.

"When you got through playin' in the water, he put clean clothes on you and a clean shirt on himself, an' by that time I'd begun to get supper. He says: 'It's too hot in here to eat comfortable. Let's have a picnic in the orchard. We'll eat our supper behind the mulberry hedge, under them linden trees.'

"So he carried our supper down, an' a bottle of my wild-grape wine, an' everything tasted good, I can tell you. The wind got cooler as the sun was goin' down, and it turned out pleasant, only I noticed how the leaves was curled up on the linden trees. That made me think, an' I asked your father if that hot wind all day hadn't been terrible hard on the gardens an' the corn.

"'Corn,' he says, 'there ain't no corn.'

"'What you talkin' about?' I said. 'Ain't we got forty acres?'

"'We ain't got an ear,' he says, 'nor nobody else ain't got none. All the corn in this country was cooked by three o'clock today, like you'd roasted it in an oven.'

"'You mean you won't get no crop at all?' I asked him. I couldn't believe it, after he'd worked so hard.

"'No crop this year,' he says. 'That's why we're havin' a picnic. We might as well enjoy what we got.'

"An' that's how your father behaved, when all the neighbours was so discouraged they couldn't look you in the face. An' we enjoyed ourselves that year, poor as we was, an' our neighbours wasn't a bit better off for bein' miserable. Some of 'em grieved till they got poor digestions and couldn't relish what they did have."

The younger boys said they thought their

father had the best of it. But Rudolf was thinking that, all the same, the neighbours had managed to get ahead more, in the fifteen years since that time. There must be something wrong about his father's way of doing things. He wished he knew what was going on in the back of Polly's mind. He knew she liked his father, but he knew, too, that she was afraid of something. When his mother sent over coffee-cake or prune tarts or a loaf of fresh bread, Polly seemed to regard them with a certain suspicion. When she observed to him that his brothers had nice manners, her tone implied that it was remarkable they should have. With his mother she was stiff and on her guard. Mary's hearty frankness and gusts of good humour irritated her. Polly was afraid of being unusual or conspicuous in any way, of being " ordinary," as she said!

When Mary had finished her story, Rosicky laid aside his pipe.

" You boys like me to tell you about some of dem hard times I been through in London? " Warmly encouraged, he sat rubbing his forehead along the deep creases. It was bothersome to tell a long story in English (he nearly always talked to the boys in Czech), but he wanted Polly to hear this one.

"Well, you know about dat tailor shop I worked in in London? I had one Christmas dere I ain't never forgot. Times was awful bad before Christmas; de boss ain't got much work, an' have it awful hard to pay his rent. It ain't so much fun, bein' poor in a big city like London, I'll say! All de windows is full of good t'ings to eat, an' all de pushcarts in de streets is full, an' you smell 'em all de time, an' you ain't got no money, — not a damn bit. I didn't mind de cold so much, though I didn't have no overcoat, chust a short jacket I'd outgrowed so it wouldn't meet on me, an' my hands was chapped raw. But I always had a good appetite, like you all know, an' de sight of dem pork pies in de windows was awful fur me!

"Day before Christmas was terrible foggy dat year, an' dat fog gits into your bones and makes you all damp like. Mrs. Lifschnitz didn't give us nothin' but a little bread an' drippin' for supper, because she was savin' to try for to give us a good dinner on Christmas Day. After supper de boss say I can go an' enjoy myself, so I went into de streets to listen to de Christmas singers. Dey sing old songs an' make very nice music, an' I run round after dem a good ways, till I got awful hungry. I t'ink maybe if I go home, I can sleep till morning an' forgit my belly.

"I went into my corner real quiet, and roll up in my fedder quilt. But I ain't got my head down, till I smell somet'ing good. Seem like it git stronger an' stronger, an' I can't git to sleep noway. I can't understand dat smell. Dere was a gas light in a hall across de court, dat always shine in at my window a little. I got up an' look round. I got a little wooden box in my corner fur a stool, 'cause I ain't got no chair. I picks up dat box, and under it dere is a roast goose on a platter! I can't believe my eyes. I carry it to de window where de light comes in, an' touch it and smell it to find out, an' den I taste it to be sure. I say, I will eat chust one little bite of dat goose, so I can go to sleep, and tomorrow I won't eat none at all. But I tell you, boys, when I stop, one half of dat goose was gone!"

The narrator bowed his head, and the boys shouted. But little Josephine slipped behind his chair and kissed him on the neck beneath his ear.

"Poor little Papa, I don't want him to be hungry!"

"Da's long ago, child. I ain't never been hungry since I had your mudder to cook fur me."

"Go on and tell us the rest, please," said Polly.

"Well, when I come to realize what I done, of course, I felt terrible. I felt better in de stomach, but very bad in de heart. I set on my bed wid dat platter on my knees, an' it all come to me; how hard dat poor woman save to buy dat goose, and how she get some neighbour to cook it dat got more fire, an' how she put it in my corner to keep it away from dem hungry children. Dey was a old carpet hung up to shut my corner off, an' de children wasn't allowed to go in dere. An' I know she put it in my corner because she trust me more'n she did de violin boy. I can't stand it to face her after I spoil de Christmas. So I put on my shoes and go out into de city. I tell myself I better throw myself in de river; but I guess I ain't dat kind of a boy.

"It was after twelve o'clock, an' terrible cold, an' I start out to walk about London all night. I walk along de river awhile, but dey was lots of drunks all along; men, and women too. I chust move along to keep away from de police. I git onto de Strand, an' den over to New Oxford Street, where dere was a big German restaurant on de ground floor, wid big windows all fixed up fine, an' I could see de people havin' parties inside. While I was lookin' in, two men and two ladies come out, laughin' and talkin' and feelin' happy about all dey been eatin' an' drinkin', and dey was speakin' Czech, — not like de Austrians, but like de home folks talk it.

"I guess I went crazy, an' I done what I ain't never done before nor since. I went right

up to dem gay people an' begun to beg dem:
'Fellow-countrymen, for God's sake give me
money enough to buy a goose!'

"Dey laugh, of course, but de ladies speak
awful kind to me, an' dey take me back into de
restaurant and give me hot coffee and cakes,
an' make me tell all about how I happened to
come to London, an' what I was doin' dere.
Dey take my name and where I work down on
paper, an' both of dem ladies give me ten
shillings.

"De big market at Covent Garden ain't
very far away, an' by dat time it was open. I
go dere an' buy a big goose an' some pork pies,
an' potatoes and onions, an' cakes an' oranges
fur de children, — all I could carry! When I
git home, everybody is still asleep. I pile all I
bought on de kitchen table, an' go in an' lay
down on my bed, an' I ain't waken up till I
hear dat woman scream when she come out into
her kitchen. My goodness, but she was surprise! She laugh an' cry at de same time, an'
hug me and waken all de children. She ain't
stop fur no breakfast; she git de Christmas

dinner ready dat morning, and we all sit down an' eat all we can hold. I ain't never seen dat violin boy have all he can hold before.

"Two three days after dat, de two men come to hunt me up, an' dey ask my boss, and he give me a good report an' tell dem I was a steady boy all right. One of dem Bohemians was very smart an' run a Bohemian newspaper in New York, an' de odder was a rich man, in de importing business, an' dey been travelling togedder. Dey told me how t'ings was easier in New York, an' offered to pay my passage when dey was goin' home soon on a boat. My boss say to me: 'You go. You ain't got no chance here, an' I like to see you git ahead, fur you always been a good boy to my woman, and fur dat fine Christmas dinner you give us all.' An' da's how I got to New York."

That night when Rudolph and Polly, arm in arm, were running home across the fields with the bitter wind at their backs, his heart leaped for joy when she said she thought they might have his family come over for supper on

New Year's Eve. "Let's get up a nice supper, and not let your mother help at all; make her be company for once."

"That would be lovely of you, Polly," he said humbly. He was a very simple, modest boy, and he, too, felt vaguely that Polly and her sisters were more experienced and worldly than his people.

VI

The winter turned out badly for farmers. It was bitterly cold, and after the first light snows before Christmas there was no snow at all, — and no rain. March was as bitter as February. On those days when the wind fairly punished the country, Rosicky sat by his window. In the fall he and the boys had put in a big wheat planting, and now the seed had frozen in the ground. All that land would have to be ploughed up and planted over again, planted in corn. It had happened before, but he was

younger then, and he never worried about
what had to be. He was sure of himself and of
Mary; he knew they could bear what they had
to bear, that they would always pull through
somehow. But he was not so sure about the
young ones, and he felt troubled because Rudolph and Polly were having such a hard start.

Sitting beside his flowering window while
the panes rattled and the wind blew in under
the door, Rosicky gave himself to reflection as
he had not done since those Sundays in the loft
of the furniture-factory in New York, long
ago. Then he was trying to find what he wanted
in life for himself; now he was trying to find
what he wanted for his boys, and why it was
he so hungered to feel sure they would be here,
working this very land, after he was gone.

They would have to work hard on the farm,
and probably they would never do much more
than make a living. But if he could think of
them as staying here on the land, he wouldn't
have to fear any great unkindness for them.
Hardships, certainly; it was a hardship to have
the wheat freeze in the ground when seed was so

high; and to have to sell your stock because you had no feed. But there would be other years when everything came along right, and you caught up. And what you had was your own. You didn't have to choose between bosses and strikers, and go wrong either way. You didn't have to do with dishonest and cruel people. They were the only things in his experience he had found terrifying and horrible; the look in the eyes of a dishonest and crafty man, of a scheming and rapacious woman.

In the country, if you had a mean neighbour, you could keep off his land and make him keep off yours. But in the city, all the foulness and misery and brutality of your neighbours was part of your life. The worst things he had come upon in his journey through the world were human, — depraved and poisonous specimens of man. To this day he could recall certain terrible faces in the London streets. There were mean people everywhere, to be sure, even in their own country town here. But they weren't tempered, hardened, sharpened, like the treacherous people in cities who live by grinding or cheating or poisoning their fellow-men. He had helped to bury two of his fellow-workmen in the tailoring trade, and he was distrustful of the organized industries that see one out of the world in big cities. Here, if you were sick, you had Doctor Ed to look after you; and if you died, fat Mr. Haycock, the kindest man in the world, buried you.

It seemed to Rosicky that for good, honest boys like his, the worst they could do on the farm was better than the best they would be likely to do in the city. If he'd had a mean boy, now, one who was crooked and sharp and tried to put anything over on his brothers, then town would be the place for him. But he had no such boy. As for Rudolph, the discontented one, he would give the shirt off his back to anyone who touched his heart. What Rosicky really hoped for his boys was that they could get through the world without ever knowing much about the cruelty of human beings. " Their mother and me ain't prepared them for that," he sometimes said to himself.

These thoughts brought him back to a grateful consideration of his own case. What an escape he had had, to be sure! He, too, in his time, had had to take money for repair work from the hand of a hungry child who let it go so wistfully; because it was money due his boss. And now, in all these years, he had never had to take a cent from anyone in bitter need, — never had to look at the face of a woman become like a wolf's from struggle and famine. When he thought of these things, Rosicky would put on his cap and jacket and slip down to the barn and give his work-horses a little extra oats, letting them eat it out of his hand in their slobbery fashion. It was his way of expressing what he felt, and made him chuckle with pleasure.

The spring came warm, with blue skies, — but dry, dry as a bone. The boys began ploughing up the wheat-fields to plant them over in corn. Rosicky would stand at the fence corner and watch them, and the earth was so dry it blew up in clouds of brown dust that hid the horses and the sulky plough and the driver. It was a bad outlook.

The big alfalfa-field that lay between the home place and Rudolph's came up green, but Rosicky was worried because during that open windy winter a great many Russian thistle plants had blown in there and lodged. He kept asking the boys to rake them out; he was afraid their seed would root and "take the alfalfa." Rudolph said that was nonsense. The boys were working so hard planting corn, their father felt he couldn't insist about the thistles, but he set great store by that big alfalfa field. It was a feed you could depend on, — and there was some deeper reason, vague, but strong. The peculiar green of that clover woke early memories in old Rosicky, went back to something in his childhood in the old world. When he was a little boy, he had played in fields of that strong blue-green colour.

One morning, when Rudolph had gone to town in the car, leaving a work-team idle in his barn, Rosicky went over to his son's place, put the horses to the buggy-rake, and set about quietly raking up those thistles. He behaved with guilty caution, and rather enjoyed stealing a march on Doctor Ed, who was just then taking his first vacation in seven years of practice and was attending a clinic in Chicago. Rosicky got the thistles raked up, but did not stop to burn them. That would take some time, and his breath was pretty short, so he thought he had better get the horses back to the barn.

He got them into the barn and to their stalls, but the pain had come on so sharp in his chest that he didn't try to take the harness off. He started for the house, bending lower with every step. The cramp in his chest was shutting him up like a jack-knife. When he reached the windmill, he swayed and caught at the ladder. He saw Polly coming down the hill, running with the swiftness of a slim greyhound. In a flash she had her shoulder under his armpit.

" Lean on me, Father, hard! Don't be afraid. We can get to the house all right."

Somehow they did, though Rosicky became blind with pain; he could keep on his legs, but he couldn't steer his course. The next thing he was conscious of was lying on Polly's bed, and

Polly bending over him wringing out bath towels in hot water and putting them on his chest. She stopped only to throw coal into the stove, and she kept the tea-kettle and the black pot going. She put these hot applications on him for nearly an hour, she told him afterwards, and all that time he was drawn up stiff and blue, with the sweat pouring off him.

As the pain gradually loosed its grip, the stiffness went out of his jaws, the black circles round his eyes disappeared, and a little of his natural colour came back. When his daughter-in-law buttoned his shirt over his chest at last, he sighed.

"Da's fine, de way I feel now, Polly. It was a awful bad spell, an' I was so sorry it all come on you like it did."

Polly was flushed and excited. "Is the pain really gone? Can I leave you long enough to telephone over to your place?"

Rosicky's eyelids fluttered. "Don't telephone, Polly. It ain't no use to scare my wife. It's nice and quiet here, an' if I ain't too much trouble to you, just let me lay still till I feel like myself. I ain't got no pain now. It's nice here."

Polly bent over him and wiped the moisture from his face. " Oh, I'm so glad it's over! " she broke out impulsively. " It just broke my heart to see you suffer so, Father."

Rosicky motioned her to sit down on the chair where the tea-kettle had been, and looked up at her with that lively affectionate gleam in his eyes. " You was awful good to me, I won't never forgit dat. I hate it to be sick on you like dis. Down at de barn I say to myself, dat young girl ain't had much experience in sickness, I don't want to scare her, an' maybe she's got a baby comin' or somet'ing."

Polly took his hand. He was looking at her so intently and affectionately and confidingly; his eyes seemed to caress her face, to regard it with pleasure. She frowned with her funny streaks of eyebrows, and then smiled back at him.

" I guess maybe there is something of that kind going to happen. But I haven't told anyone yet, not my mother or Rudolph. You'll be the first to know."

His hand pressed hers. She noticed that it was warm again. The twinkle in his yellow-brown eyes seemed to come nearer.

"I like mighty well to see dat little child, Polly," was all he said. Then he closed his eyes and lay half-smiling. But Polly sat still, thinking hard. She had a sudden feeling that nobody in the world, not her mother, not Rudolph, or anyone, really loved her as much as old Rosicky did. It perplexed her. She sat frowning and trying to puzzle it out. It was as if Rosicky had a special gift for loving people, something that was like an ear for music or an eye for colour. It was quiet, unobtrusive; it was merely there. You saw it in his eyes, — perhaps that was why they were merry. You felt it in his hands, too. After he dropped off to sleep, she sat holding his warm, broad, flexible brown hand. She had never seen another in the least like it. She wondered if it wasn't a kind of gypsy hand, it was so alive and quick and light in its communications, — very strange in a farmer. Nearly all the farmers she knew had huge lumps of fists, like mauls, or they were knotty and bony and uncomfortable-looking, with stiff fingers. But Rosicky's was like quick-silver, flexible, muscular, about the colour of a pale cigar, with deep, deep creases across the palm. It wasn't nervous, it wasn't a stupid lump; it was a warm brown human hand, with some cleverness in it, a great deal of generosity, and something else which Polly could only call "gypsy-like,"—something nimble and lively and sure, in the way that animals are.

Polly remembered that hour long afterwards; it had been like an awakening to her. It seemed to her that she had never learned so much about life from anything as from old Rosicky's hand. It brought her to herself; it communicated some direct and untranslatable message.

When she heard Rudolph coming in the car, she ran out to meet him.

"Oh, Rudy, your father's been awful sick! He raked up those thistles he's been worrying about, and afterwards he could hardly get to the house. He suffered so I was afraid he was going to die."

Rudolph jumped to the ground. "Where is he now?"

"On the bed. He's asleep. I was terribly scared, because, you know, I'm so fond of your father." She slipped her arm through his and they went into the house. That afternoon they took Rosicky home and put him to bed, though he protested that he was quite well again.

The next morning he got up and dressed and sat down to breakfast with his family. He told Mary that his coffee tasted better than usual to him, and he warned the boys not to bear any tales to Doctor Ed when he got home. After breakfast he sat down by his window to do some patching and asked Mary to thread several needles for him before she went to feed her chickens, — her eyes were better than his, and her hands steadier. He lit his pipe and took up John's overalls. Mary had been watching him anxiously all morning, and as she went out of the door with her bucket of scraps, she saw that he was smiling. He was thinking, indeed, about Polly, and how he might never have known what a tender heart she had if he hadn't got sick over there. Girls nowadays didn't wear their heart on their sleeve. But now he knew Polly would make a fine woman after the foolishness wore off. Either a woman had that sweetness at her heart or she hadn't. You couldn't always tell by the look of them; but if they had that, everything came out right in the end.

After he had taken a few stitches, the cramp began in his chest, like yesterday. He put his pipe cautiously down on the window-sill and bent over to ease the pull. No use, — he had better try to get to his bed if he could. He rose and groped his way across the familiar floor, which was rising and falling like the deck of a ship. At the door he fell. When Mary came in, she found him lying there, and the moment she touched him she knew that he was gone.

Doctor Ed was away when Rosicky died, and for the first few weeks after he got home he was hard driven. Every day he said to himself that he must get out to see that family that had lost their father. One soft, warm

moonlight night in early summer he started for
the farm. His mind was on other things, and
not until his road ran by the graveyard did he
realize that Rosicky wasn't over there on the
hill where the red lamplight shone, but here, in
the moonlight. He stopped his car, shut off the
engine, and sat there for a while.

A sudden hush had fallen on his soul. Everything here seemed strangely moving and sig-
nificant, though signifying what, he did not
know. Close by the wire fence stood Rosicky's
mowing-machine, where one of the boys had
been cutting hay that afternoon; his own work-
horses had been going up and down there. The
new-cut hay perfumed all the night air. The
moonlight silvered the long, billowy grass that
grew over the graves and hid the fence; the few
little evergreens stood out black in it, like shadows in a pool. The sky was very blue and soft,
the stars rather faint because the moon was full.

For the first time it struck Doctor Ed that
this was really a beautiful graveyard. He
thought of city cemeteries; acres of shrubbery
and heavy stone, so arranged and lonely and

unlike anything in the living world. Cities of the dead, indeed; cities of the forgotten, of the " put away." But this was open and free, this little square of long grass which the wind for ever stirred. Nothing but the sky overhead, and the many-coloured fields running on until they met that sky. The horses worked here in summer; the neighbours passed on their way to town; and over yonder, in the cornfield, Rosicky's own cattle would be eating fodder as winter came on. Nothing could be more undeathlike than this place; nothing could be more right for a man who had helped to do the work of great cities and had always longed for the open country and had got to it at last. Rosicky's life seemed to him complete and beautiful.

New York, 1928

OLD MRS. HARRIS

OLD MRS. HARRIS

I

Mrs. David Rosen, cross-stitch in hand, sat looking out of the window across her own green lawn to the ragged, sunburned back yard of her neighbours on the right. Occasionally she glanced anxiously over her shoulder toward her shining kitchen, with a black and white linoleum floor in big squares, like a marble pavement.

"Will dat woman never go?" she muttered impatiently, just under her breath. She spoke with a slight accent — it affected only her *th's,* and, occasionally, the letter *v.* But people in Skyline thought this unfortunate, in a woman whose superiority they recognized.

Mrs. Rosen ran out to move the sprinkler

to another spot on the lawn, and in doing so she saw what she had been waiting to see. From the house next door a tall, handsome woman emerged, dressed in white broadcloth and a hat with white lilacs; she carried a sunshade and walked with a free, energetic step, as if she were going out on a pleasant errand.

Mrs. Rosen darted quickly back into the house, lest her neighbour should hail her and stop to talk. She herself was in her kitchen housework dress, a crisp blue chambray which fitted smoothly over her tightly corseted figure, and her lustrous black hair was done in two smooth braids, wound flat at the back of her head, like a braided rug. She did not stop for a hat — her dark, ruddy, salmon-tinted skin had little to fear from the sun. She opened the half-closed oven door and took out a symmetrically plaited coffee-cake, beautifully browned, delicately peppered over with poppy seeds, with sugary margins about the twists. On the kitchen table a tray stood ready with cups and saucers. She wrapped the cake in a napkin, snatched up a little French coffee-pot with a black wooden handle, and ran across her green lawn, through the alley-way and the sandy, unkept yard next door, and entered her neighbour's house by the kitchen.

The kitchen was hot and empty, full of the untempered afternoon sun. A door stood open into the next room; a cluttered, hideous room, yet somehow homely. There, beside a goods-box covered with figured oilcloth, stood an old woman in a brown calico dress, washing her hot face and neck at a tin basin. She stood with her feet wide apart, in an attitude of profound weariness. She started guiltily as the visitor entered.

"Don't let me disturb you, Grandma," called Mrs. Rosen. "I always have my coffee at dis hour in the afternoon. I was just about to sit down to it when I thought: 'I will run over and see if Grandma Harris won't take a cup with me.' I hate to drink my coffee alone."

Grandma looked troubled, — at a loss. She folded her towel and concealed it behind a curtain hung across the corner of the room to make a poor sort of closet. The old lady was always composed in manner, but it was clear that she felt embarrassment.

"Thank you, Mrs. Rosen. What a pity Victoria just this minute went down town!"

"But dis time I came to see you yourself, Grandma. Don't let me disturb you. Sit down there in your own rocker, and I will put my tray on this little chair between us, so!"

Mrs. Harris sat down in her black wooden rocking-chair with curved arms and a faded cretonne pillow on the wooden seat. It stood in the corner beside a narrow spindle-frame lounge. She looked on silently while Mrs. Rosen uncovered the cake and delicately broke it with her plump, smooth, dusky-red hands. The old lady did not seem pleased, — seemed uncertain and apprehensive, indeed. But she was not fussy or fidgety. She had the kind of quiet, intensely quiet, dignity that comes from complete resignation to the chances of life. She watched Mrs. Rosen's deft hands out of grave, steady brown eyes.

"Dis is Mr. Rosen's favourite coffee-cake, Grandma, and I want you to try it. You are

such a good cook yourself, I would like your
opinion of my cake."

"It's very nice, ma'am," said Mrs. Harris
politely, but without enthusiasm.

"And you aren't drinking your coffee; do
you like more cream in it?"

"No, thank you. I'm letting it cool a little.
I generally drink it that way."

"Of course she does," thought Mrs. Rosen,
"since she never has her coffee until all the
family are done breakfast!"

Mrs. Rosen had brought Grandma Harris
coffee-cake time and again, but she knew that
Grandma merely tasted it and saved it for her
daughter Victoria, who was as fond of sweets
as her own children, and jealous about them,
moreover, — couldn't bear that special dainties
should come into the house for anyone but herself. Mrs. Rosen, vexed at her failures, had de-
termined that just once she would take a cake
to " de old lady Harris," and with her own eyes
see her eat it. The result was not all she had
hoped. Receiving a visitor alone, unsupervised
by her daughter, having cake and coffee that

should properly be saved for Victoria, was all
so irregular that Mrs. Harris could not enjoy
it. Mrs. Rosen doubted if she tasted the cake
as she swallowed it, — certainly she ate it without relish, as a hollow form. But Mrs. Rosen
enjoyed her own cake, at any rate, and she was
glad of an opportunity to sit quietly and look
at Grandmother, who was more interesting to
her than the handsome Victoria.

It was a queer place to be having coffee,
when Mrs. Rosen liked order and comeliness so
much: a hideous, cluttered room, furnished
with a rocking-horse, a sewing-machine, an
empty baby-buggy. A walnut table stood
against a blind window, piled high with old
magazines and tattered books, and children's
caps and coats. There was a wash-stand (two
wash-stands, if you counted the oilcloth-
covered box as one). A corner of the room was
curtained off with some black-and-red-striped
cotton goods, for a clothes closet. In another
corner was the wooden lounge with a thin mattress and a red calico spread which was Grandma's bed. Beside it was her wooden rocking-

chair, and the little splint-bottom chair with the legs sawed short on which her darning-basket usually stood, but which Mrs. Rosen was now using for a tea-table.

The old lady was always impressive, Mrs. Rosen was thinking, — one could not say why. Perhaps it was the way she held her head, — so simply, unprotesting and unprotected; or the gravity of her large, deep-set brown eyes, a warm, reddish brown, though their look, always direct, seemed to ask nothing and hope for nothing. They were not cold, but inscrutable, with no kindling gleam of intercourse in them. There was the kind of nobility about her head that there is about an old lion's: an absence of self-consciousness, vanity, preoccupation — something absolute. Her grey hair was parted in the middle, wound in two little horns over her ears, and done in a little flat knot behind. Her mouth was large and composed, — resigned, the corners drooping. Mrs. Rosen had very seldom heard her laugh (and then it was a gentle, polite laugh which meant only politeness). But she had observed that whenever Mrs. Harris's grandchildren were about, tumbling all over her, asking for cookies, teasing her to read to them, the old lady looked happy.

As she drank her coffee, Mrs. Rosen tried one subject after another to engage Mrs. Harris's attention.

"Do you feel this hot weather, Grandma? I am afraid you are over the stove too much. Let those naughty children have a cold lunch occasionally."

"No'm, I don't mind the heat. It's apt to come on like this for a spell in May. I don't feel the stove. I'm accustomed to it."

"Oh, so am I! But I get very impatient with my cooking in hot weather. Do you miss your old home in Tennessee very much, Grandma?"

"No'm, I can't say I do. Mr. Templeton thought Colorado was a better place to bring up the children."

"But you had things much more comfortable down there, I'm sure. These little wooden houses are too hot in summer."

" Yes'm, we were more comfortable. We had more room."

" And a flower-garden, and beautiful old trees, Mrs. Templeton told me."

" Yes'm, we had a great deal of shade."

Mrs. Rosen felt that she was not getting anywhere. She almost believed that Grandma thought she had come on an equivocal errand, to spy out something in Victoria's absence. Well, perhaps she had! Just for once she would like to get past the others to the real grandmother, — and the real grandmother was on her guard, as always. At this moment she heard a faint miaow. Mrs. Harris rose, lifting herself by the wooden arms of her chair, said: " Excuse me," went into the kitchen, and opened the screen door.

In walked a large, handsome, thickly furred Maltese cat, with long whiskers and yellow eyes and a white star on his breast. He preceded Grandmother, waited until she sat down. Then he sprang up into her lap and settled himself comfortably in the folds of her full-gathered calico skirt. He rested his chin in his deep

bluish fur and regarded Mrs. Rosen. It struck
her that he held his head in just the way
Grandmother held hers. And Grandmother
now became more alive, as if some missing part
of herself were restored.

"This is Blue Boy," she said, stroking him.
"In winter, when the screen door ain't on, he
lets himself in. He stands up on his hind legs
and presses the thumb-latch with his paw, and
just walks in like anybody."

"He's your cat, isn't he, Grandma?" Mrs.
Rosen couldn't help prying just a little; if she
could find but a single thing that was Grandma's own!

"He's our cat," replied Mrs. Harris.
"We're all very fond of him. I expect he's
Vickie's more'n anybody's."

"Of course!" groaned Mrs. Rosen to herself. "Dat Vickie is her mother over again."

Here Mrs. Harris made her first unsolicited
remark. "If you was to be troubled with mice
at any time, Mrs. Rosen, ask one of the boys
to bring Blue Boy over to you, and he'll
clear them out. He's a master mouser." She

scratched the thick blue fur at the back of his neck, and he began a deep purring. Mrs. Harris smiled. " We call that spinning, back with us. Our children still say: ' Listen to Blue Boy spin,' though none of 'em is ever heard a spinning-wheel — except maybe Vickie remembers."

"Did you have a spinning-wheel in your own house, Grandma Harris?"

" Yes'm. Miss Sadie Crummer used to come and spin for us. She was left with no home of her own, and it was to give her something to do, as much as anything, that we had her. I spun a good deal myself, in my young days." Grandmother stopped and put her hands on the arms of her chair, as if to rise. " Did you hear a door open? It might be Victoria."

" No, it was the wind shaking the screen door. Mrs. Templeton won't be home yet. She is probably in my husband's store this minute, ordering him about. All the merchants down town will take anything from your daughter. She is very popular wid de gentlemen, Grandma."

Mrs. Harris smiled complacently. "Yes'm. Victoria was always much admired."

At this moment a chorus of laughter broke in upon the warm silence, and a host of children, as it seemed to Mrs. Rosen, ran through the yard. The hand-pump on the back porch, outside the kitchen door, began to scrape and gurgle.

"It's the children, back from school," said Grandma. "They are getting a cool drink."

"But where is the baby, Grandma?"

"Vickie took Hughie in his cart over to Mr. Holliday's yard, where she studies. She's right good about minding him."

Mrs. Rosen was glad to hear that Vickie was good for something.

Three little boys came running in through the kitchen; the twins, aged ten, and Ronald, aged six, who went to kindergarten. They snatched off their caps and threw their jackets and school bags on the table, the sewing-machine, the rocking-horse.

"Howdy do, Mrs. Rosen." They spoke to her nicely. They had nice voices, nice faces, and were always courteous, like their father. "We are going to play in our back yard with some of the boys, Gram'ma," said one of the twins respectfully, and they ran out to join a troop of schoolmates who were already shouting and racing over that poor trampled back yard, strewn with velocipedes and croquet mallets and toy wagons, which was such an eyesore to Mrs. Rosen.

Mrs. Rosen got up and took her tray.

"Can't you stay a little, ma'am? Victoria will be here any minute."

But her tone let Mrs. Rosen know that Grandma really wished her to leave before Victoria returned.

A few moments after Mrs. Rosen had put the tray down in her own kitchen, Victoria Templeton came up the wooden sidewalk, attended by Mr. Rosen, who had quitted his store half an hour earlier than usual for the pleasure of walking home with her. Mrs. Templeton stopped by the picket fence to smile at the children playing in the back yard, — and it was a real smile, she was glad to see them.

She called Ronald over to the fence to give him a kiss. He was hot and sticky.

"Was your teacher nice today? Now run in and ask Grandma to wash your face and put a clean waist on you."

II

That night Mrs. Harris got supper with an effort — had to drive herself harder than usual. Mandy, the bound girl they had brought with them from the South, noticed that the old lady was uncertain and short of breath. The hours from two to four, when Mrs. Harris usually rested, had not been at all restful this afternoon. There was an understood rule that Grandmother was not to receive visitors alone. Mrs. Rosen's call, and her cake and coffee, were too much out of the accepted order. Nervousness had prevented the old lady from getting any repose during her visit.

After the rest of the family had left the supper table, she went into the dining-room and took her place, but she ate very little. She put away the food that was left, and then, while Mandy washed the dishes, Grandma sat down in her rocking-chair in the dark and dozed.

The three little boys came in from playing under the electric light (arc lights had been but lately installed in Skyline) and began begging Mrs. Harris to read *Tom Sawyer* to them. Grandmother loved to read, anything at all, the Bible or the continued story in the Chicago weekly paper. She roused herself, lit her brass " safety lamp," and pulled her black rocker out of its corner to the wash-stand (the table was too far away from her corner, and anyhow it was completely covered with coats and school satchels). She put on her old-fashioned silver-rimmed spectacles and began to read. Ronald lay down on Grandmother's lounge bed, and the twins, Albert and Adelbert, called Bert and Del, sat down against the wall, one on a low box covered with felt, and the other on the little sawed-off chair upon which Mrs. Rosen had served coffee. They looked intently at Mrs. Harris, and she looked intently at the book.

Presently Vickie, the oldest grandchild, came in. She was fifteen. Her mother was entertaining callers in the parlour, callers who didn't interest Vickie, so she was on her way up to her own room by the kitchen stairway.

Mrs. Harris looked up over her glasses. "Vickie, maybe you'd take the book awhile, and I can do my darning."

"All right," said Vickie. Reading aloud was one of the things she would always do toward the general comfort. She sat down by the washstand and went on with the story. Grandmother got her darning-basket and began to drive her needle across great knee-holes in the boys' stockings. Sometimes she nodded for a moment, and her hands fell into her lap. After a while the little boy on the lounge went to sleep. But the twins sat upright, their hands on their knees, their round brown eyes fastened upon Vickie, and when there was anything funny, they giggled. They were chubby, dark-skinned little boys, with round jolly faces, white teeth, and yellow-brown eyes that were always bubbling with fun unless they were sad, — even then their eyes never got red or weepy. Their tears sparkled and fell; left no trace but a streak on the cheeks, perhaps.

Presently old Mrs. Harris gave out a long snore of utter defeat. She had been overcome at last. Vickie put down the book. "That's enough for tonight. Grandmother's sleepy, and Ronald's fast asleep. What'll we do with him?"

"Bert and me'll get him undressed," said Adelbert. The twins roused the sleepy little boy and prodded him up the back stairway to the bare room without window blinds, where he was put into his cot beside their double bed. Vickie's room was across the narrow hallway; not much bigger than a closet, but, anyway, it was her own. She had a chair and an old dresser, and beside her bed was a high stool which she used as a lamp-table, — she always read in bed.

After Vickie went upstairs, the house was quiet. Hughie, the baby, was asleep in his mother's room, and Victoria herself, who still treated her husband as if he were her " beau," had persuaded him to take her down town to the ice-cream parlour. Grandmother's room, between the kitchen and the dining-room, was rather like a passage-way; but now that the children were upstairs and Victoria was off enjoying herself somewhere, Mrs. Harris could be sure of enough privacy to undress. She took off the calico cover from her lounge bed and folded it up, put on her nightgown and white nightcap.

Mandy, the bound girl, appeared at the kitchen door.

" Miz' Harris," she said in a guarded tone, ducking her head, " you want me to rub your feet for you? "

For the first time in the long day the old woman's low composure broke a little. " Oh, Mandy, I would take it kindly of you! " she breathed gratefully.

That had to be done in the kitchen; Victoria didn't like anybody slopping about. Mrs. Harris put an old checked shawl round her shoulders and followed Mandy. Beside the kitchen stove Mandy had a little wooden tub full of warm water. She knelt down and untied Mrs. Harris's garter strings and took off her flat cloth slippers and stockings.

"Oh, Miz' Harris, your feet an' legs is swelled turrible tonight!"

"I expect they air, Mandy. They feel like it."

"Pore soul!" murmured Mandy. She put Grandma's feet in the tub and, crouching beside it, slowly, slowly rubbed her swollen legs. Mandy was tired, too. Mrs. Harris sat in her nightcap and shawl, her hands crossed in her lap. She never asked for this greatest solace of the day; it was something that Mandy gave, who had nothing else to give. If there could be a comparison in absolutes, Mandy was the needier of the two, — but she was younger. The kitchen was quiet and full of shadow, with only the light from an old lantern. Neither spoke. Mrs. Harris dozed from comfort, and Mandy herself was half asleep as she performed one of the oldest rites of compassion.

OLD MRS. HARRIS

Although Mrs. Harris's lounge had no springs, only a thin cotton mattress between her and the wooden slats, she usually went to sleep as soon as she was in bed. To be off her feet, to lie flat, to say over the psalm beginning: *"The Lord is my shepherd,"* was comfort enough. About four o'clock in the morning, however, she would begin to feel the hard slats under her, and the heaviness of the old home-made quilts, with weight but little warmth, on top of her. Then she would reach under her pillow for her little comforter (she called it that to herself) that Mrs. Rosen had given her. It was a tan sweater of very soft brushed wool, with one sleeve torn and ragged. A young nephew from Chicago had spent a fortnight with Mrs. Rosen last summer and had left this behind him. One morning, when Mrs. Harris went out to the stable at the back of the yard to pat Buttercup, the cow, Mrs. Rosen ran across the alley-way.

"Grandma Harris," she said, coming into the shelter of the stable, "I wonder if you could make any use of this sweater Sammy left? The yarn might be good for your darning."

Mrs. Harris felt of the article gravely. Mrs. Rosen thought her face brightened. " Yes'm, indeed I could use it. I thank you kindly."

She slipped it under her apron, carried it into the house with her, and concealed it under her mattress. There she had kept it ever since. She knew Mrs. Rosen understood how it was; that Victoria couldn't bear to have anything come into the house that was not for her to dispose of.

On winter nights, and even on summer nights after the cocks began to crow, Mrs. Harris often felt cold and lonely about the chest. Sometimes her cat, Blue Boy, would creep in beside her and warm that aching spot. But on spring and summer nights he was likely to be abroad skylarking, and this little sweater had become the dearest of Grandmother's few possessions. It was kinder to her, she used to think, as she wrapped it about her middle, than any of her own children had been. She had married at eighteen and had had eight children; but some died, and some were, as she said, scattered.

After she was warm in that tender spot under the ribs, the old woman could lie patiently on the slats, waiting for daybreak; thinking about the comfortable rambling old house in Tennessee, its feather beds and hand-woven rag carpets and splint-bottom chairs, the mahogany sideboard, and the marble-top parlour table; all that she had left behind to follow Victoria's fortunes.

She did not regret her decision; indeed, there had been no decision. Victoria had never once thought it possible that Ma should not go wherever she and the children went, and Mrs. Harris had never thought it possible. Of course she regretted Tennessee, though she would never admit it to Mrs. Rosen: — the old neighbours, the yard and garden she had worked in all her life, the apple trees she had planted, the lilac arbour, tall enough to walk in, which she had clipped and shaped so many years. Especially she missed her lemon tree, in a tub on the front porch, which bore little lemons almost every summer, and folks would come for miles to see it.

But the road had led westward, and Mrs. Harris didn't believe that women, especially old women, could say when or where they would stop. They were tied to the chariot of young life, and had to go where it went, because they were needed. Mrs. Harris had gathered from Mrs. Rosen's manner, and from comments she occasionally dropped, that the Jewish people had an altogether different attitude toward their old folks; therefore her friendship with this kind neighbour was almost as disturbing as it was pleasant. She didn't want Mrs. Rosen to think that she was " put upon," that there was anything unusual or pitiful in her lot. To be pitied was the deepest hurt anybody could know. And if Victoria once suspected Mrs. Rosen's indignation, it would be all over. She would freeze her neighbour out, and that friendly voice, that quick pleasant chatter with the little foreign twist, would thenceforth be heard only at a distance, in the alley-way or across the fence. Victoria had a good heart, but she was terribly proud and could not bear the least criticism.

As soon as the grey light began to steal into the room, Mrs. Harris would get up softly and wash at the basin on the oilcloth-covered box. She would wet her hair above her forehead, comb it with a little bone comb set in a tin rim, do it up in two smooth little horns over her ears, wipe the comb dry, and put it away in the pocket of her full-gathered calico skirt. She left nothing lying about. As soon as she was dressed, she made her bed, folding her nightgown and nightcap under the pillow, the sweater under the mattress. She smoothed the heavy quilts, and drew the red calico spread neatly over all. Her towel was hung on its special nail behind the curtain. Her soap she kept in a tin tobacco-box; the children's soap was in a crockery saucer. If her soap or towel got mixed up with the children's, Victoria was always sharp about it. The little rented house was much too small for the family, and Mrs. Harris and her " things " were almost required to be invisible. Two clean calico dresses hung in the curtained corner; another was on her back, and a fourth was in the wash. Behind the curtain there was always a good supply of aprons; Victoria bought them at church fairs, and it was a great satisfaction to Mrs. Harris to put on a clean one whenever she liked. Upstairs, in Mandy's attic room over the kitchen, hung a black cashmere dress and a black bonnet with a long crêpe veil, for the rare occasions when Mr. Templeton hired a double buggy and horses and drove his family to a picnic or to Decoration Day exercises. Mrs. Harris rather dreaded these drives, for Victoria was usually cross afterwards.

When Mrs. Harris went out into the kitchen to get breakfast, Mandy always had the fire started and the water boiling. They enjoyed a quiet half-hour before the little boys came running down the stairs, always in a good humour. In winter the boys had their breakfast in the kitchen, with Vickie. Mrs. Harris made Mandy eat the cakes and fried ham the children left, so that she would not fast so long. Mr. and Mrs. Templeton breakfasted rather late, in the dining-room, and they always had fruit and thick cream, — a small pitcher of the very thickest was for Mrs. Templeton. The children were never fussy about their food. As Grandmother often said feelingly to Mrs. Rosen, they were as little trouble as children could possibly be. They sometimes tore their clothes, of course, or got sick. But even when Albert had an abscess in his ear and was in such pain, he would lie for hours on Grandmother's lounge with his cheek on a bag of hot salt, if only she or Vickie would read aloud to him.

"It's true, too, what de old lady says," remarked Mrs. Rosen to her husband one night at supper, " dey are nice children. No one ever taught them anything, but they have good instincts, even dat Vickie. And think, if you please, of all the self-sacrificing mothers we know, — Fannie and Esther, to come near home; how they have planned for those children from infancy and given them every advantage. And now ingratitude and coldness is what dey meet with."

Mr. Rosen smiled his teasing smile. " Evidently your sister and mine have the wrong method. The way to make your children unselfish is to be comfortably selfish yourself."

" But dat woman takes no more responsibility for her children than a cat takes for her kittens. Nor does poor young Mr. Templeton, for dat matter. How can he expect to get so many children started in life, I ask you? It is not at all fair! "

Mr. Rosen sometimes had to hear altogether too much about the Templetons, but he was patient, because it was a bitter sorrow to Mrs. Rosen that she had no children. There was nothing else in the world she wanted so much.

III

Mrs. Rosen in one of her blue working dresses, the indigo blue that became a dark skin and dusky red cheeks with a tone of salmon colour, was in her shining kitchen, washing her beautiful dishes — her neighbours often wondered why she used her best china and linen every day — when Vickie Templeton came in with a book under her arm.

"Good day, Mrs. Rosen. Can I have the second volume?"

"Certainly. You know where the books are." She spoke coolly, for it always annoyed her that Vickie never suggested wiping the dishes or helping with such household work as happened to be going on when she dropped in. She hated the girl's bringing-up so much that sometimes she almost hated the girl.

Vickie strolled carelessly through the dining-room into the parlour and opened the doors of one of the big bookcases. Mr. Rosen had a large library, and a great many unusual books. There was a complete set of the Waverley Novels in German, for example; thick, dumpy little volumes bound in tooled leather, with very black type and dramatic engravings printed on wrinkled, yellowing pages. There were many French books, and some of the German classics done into English, such as Coleridge's translation of Schiller's *Wallenstein.*

Of course no other house in Skyline was in the least like Mrs. Rosen's; it was the nearest thing to an art gallery and a museum that the Templetons had ever seen. All the rooms were carpeted alike (that was very unusual), with a soft velvet carpet, little blue and rose flowers scattered on a rose-grey ground. The deep chairs were upholstered in dark blue velvet. The walls were hung with engravings in pale gold frames: some of Raphael's "Hours," a large soft engraving of a castle on the Rhine, and another of cypress trees about a Roman ruin, under a full moon. There were a number of water-colour sketches, made in Italy by Mr. Rosen himself when he was a boy. A rich uncle had taken him abroad as his secretary. Mr. Rosen was a reflective, unambitious man, who didn't mind keeping a clothing-store in a little Western town, so long as he had a great deal of time to read philosophy. He was the only unsuccessful member of a large, rich Jewish family.

Last August, when the heat was terrible in Skyline, and the crops were burned up on all

the farms to the north, and the wind from the
pink and yellow sand-hills to the south blew
so hot that it singed the few green lawns in
the town, Vickie had taken to dropping in
upon Mrs. Rosen at the very hottest part of
the afternoon. Mrs. Rosen knew, of course,
that it was probably because the girl had no
other cool and quiet place to go — her room
at home under the roof would be hot enough!
Now, Mrs. Rosen liked to undress and take a
nap from three to five, — if only to get out of
her tight corsets, for she would have an hour-
glass figure at any cost. She told Vickie firmly
that she was welcome to come if she would read
in the parlour with the blind up only a little
way, and would be as still as a mouse. Vickie
came, meekly enough, but she seldom read. She
would take a sofa pillow and lie down on the
soft carpet and look up at the pictures in the
dusky room, and feel a happy, pleasant excitement from the heat and glare outside and
the deep shadow and quiet within. Curiously
enough, Mrs. Rosen's house never made her

dissatisfied with her own; she thought that very nice, too.

Mrs. Rosen, leaving her kitchen in a state of such perfection as the Templetons were unable to sense or to admire, came into the parlour and found her visitor sitting cross-legged on the floor before one of the bookcases.

" Well, Vickie, and how did you get along with *Wilhelm Meister*? "

" I like it," said Vickie.

Mrs. Rosen shrugged. The Templetons always said that; quite as if a book or a cake were lucky to win their approbation.

" Well, *what* did you like? "

" I guess I liked all that about the theatre and Shakspere best."

" It's rather celebrated," remarked Mrs. Rosen dryly. " And are you studying every day? Do you think you will be able to win that scholarship? "

" I don't know. I'm going to try awful hard."

Mrs. Rosen wondered whether any Templeton knew how to try very hard. She reached for her work-basket and began to do cross-stitch. It made her nervous to sit with folded hands.

Vickie was looking at a German book in her lap, an illustrated edition of *Faust*. She had stopped at a very German picture of Gretchen entering the church, with Faustus gazing at her from behind a rose tree, Mephisto at his shoulder.

"I wish I could read this," she said, frowning at the black Gothic text. "It's splendid, isn't it?"

Mrs. Rosen rolled her eyes upward and sighed. "Oh, my dear, one of de world's masterpieces!"

That meant little to Vickie. She had not been taught to respect masterpieces, she had no scale of that sort in her mind. She cared about a book only because it took hold of her.

She kept turning over the pages. Between the first and second parts, in this edition, there was inserted the *Dies Iræ* hymn in full. She stopped and puzzled over it for a long while.

"Here is something I can read," she said, showing the page to Mrs. Rosen.

Mrs. Rosen looked up from her cross-stitch. "There you have the advantage of me. I do not read Latin. You might translate it for me."

Vickie began:

> "Day of wrath, upon that day
> The world to ashes melts away,
> As David and the Sibyl say.

"But that don't give you the rhyme; every line ought to end in two syllables."

"Never mind if it doesn't give the metre," corrected Mrs. Rosen kindly; "go on, if you can."

Vickie went on stumbling through the Latin verses, and Mrs. Rosen sat watching her. You couldn't tell about Vickie. She wasn't pretty, yet Mrs. Rosen found her attractive. She liked her sturdy build and the steady vitality that glowed in her rosy skin and dark blue eyes, — even gave a springy quality to her curly reddish-brown hair, which she still wore in a single braid down her back. Mrs. Rosen liked to have

Vickie about because she was never listless or dreamy or apathetic. A half-smile nearly always played about her lips and eyes, and it was there because she was pleased with something, not because she wanted to be agreeable. Even a half-smile made her cheeks dimple. She had what her mother called "a happy disposition."

When she finished the verses, Mrs. Rosen nodded approvingly. "Thank you, Vickie. The very next time I go to Chicago, I will try to get an English translation of *Faust* for you."

"But I want to read this one." Vickie's open smile darkened. "What I want is to pick up any of these books and just read them, like you and Mr. Rosen do."

The dusky red of Mrs. Rosen's cheeks grew a trifle deeper. Vickie never paid compliments, absolutely never; but if she really admired anyone, something in her voice betrayed it so convincingly that one felt flattered. When she dropped a remark of this kind, she added another link to the chain of responsibility which

Mrs. Rosen unwillingly bore and tried to shake off — the irritating sense of being somehow responsible for Vickie, since, God knew, no one else felt responsible.

Once or twice, when she happened to meet pleasant young Mr. Templeton alone, she had tried to talk to him seriously about his daughter's future. " She has finished de school here, and she should be getting training of some sort; she is growing up," she told him severely.

He laughed and said in his way that was so honest, and so disarmingly sweet and frank: " Oh, don't remind me, Mrs. Rosen! I just pretend to myself she isn't. I want to keep my little daughter as long as I can." And there it ended.

Sometimes Vickie Templeton seemed so dense, so utterly unperceptive, that Mrs. Rosen was ready to wash her hands of her. Then some queer streak of sensibility in the child would make her change her mind. Last winter, when Mrs. Rosen came home from a visit to her sister in Chicago, she brought with her a new cloak of the sleeveless dolman type, black velvet, lined with grey and white squirrel skins, a grey skin next a white. Vickie, so indifferent to clothes, fell in love with that cloak. Her eyes followed it with delight whenever Mrs. Rosen wore it. She found it picturesque, romantic. Mrs. Rosen had been captivated by the same thing in the cloak, and had bought it with a shrug, knowing it would be quite out of place in Skyline; and Mr. Rosen, when she first produced it from her trunk, had laughed and said: "Where did you get that? — out of *Rigoletto*?" It looked like that — but how could Vickie know?

Vickie's whole family puzzled Mrs. Rosen; their feelings were so much finer than their way of living. She bought milk from the Templetons because they kept a cow — which Mandy milked, — and every night one of the twins brought the milk to her in a tin pail. Whichever boy brought it, she always called him Albert — she thought Adelbert a silly, Southern name.

One night when she was fitting the lid on an empty pail, she said severely:

"Now, Albert, I have put some cookies for Grandma in this pail, wrapped in a napkin. And they are for Grandma, remember, not for your mother or Vickie."

"Yes'm."

When she turned to him to give him the pail, she saw two full crystal globes in the little boy's eyes, just ready to break. She watched him go softly down the path and dash those tears away with the back of his hand. She was sorry. She hadn't thought the little boys realized that their household was somehow a queer one.

Queer or not, Mrs. Rosen liked to go there better than to most houses in the town. There was something easy, cordial, and carefree in the parlour that never smelled of being shut up, and the ugly furniture looked hospitable. One felt a pleasantness in the human relationships. These people didn't seem to know there were such things as struggle or exactness or competition in the world. They were always genuinely glad to see you, had time to see you, and were usually gay in mood — all but

Grandmother, who had the kind of gravity that people who take thought of human destiny must have. But even she liked light-heartedness in others; she drudged, indeed, to keep it going.

There were houses that were better kept, certainly, but the housekeepers had no charm, no gentleness of manner, were like hard little machines, most of them; and some were grasping and narrow. The Templetons were not selfish or scheming. Anyone could take advantage of them, and many people did. Victoria might eat all the cookies her neighbour sent in, but she would give away anything she had. She was always ready to lend her dresses and hats and bits of jewellery for the school theatricals, and she never worked people for favours.

As for Mr. Templeton (people usually called him " young Mr. Templeton "), he was too delicate to collect his just debts. His boyish, eager-to-please manner, his fair complexion and blue eyes and young face, made him seem very soft to some of the hard old money-grubbers on Main Street, and the fact

that he always said " Yes, sir," and " No, sir,"
to men older than himself furnished a good
deal of amusement to by-standers.

Two years ago, when this Templeton family
came to Skyline and moved into the house next
door, Mrs. Rosen was inconsolable. The new
neighbours had a lot of children, who would
always be making a racket. They put a cow
and a horse into the empty barn, which would
mean dirt and flies. They strewed their back
yard with packing-cases and did not pick
them up.

She first met Mrs. Templeton at an afternoon card party, in a house at the extreme north
end of the town, fully half a mile away, and
she had to admit that her new neighbour was
an attractive woman, and that there was something warm and genuine about her. She wasn't
in the least willowy or languishing, as Mrs.
Rosen had usually found Southern ladies to
be. She was high-spirited and direct; a trifle
imperious, but with a shade of diffidence,
too, as if she were trying to adjust herself to

a new group of people and to do the right thing.

While they were at the party, a blinding snowstorm came on, with a hard wind. Since they lived next door to each other, Mrs. Rosen and Mrs. Templeton struggled homeward together through the blizzard. Mrs. Templeton seemed delighted with the rough weather; she laughed like a big country girl whenever she made a mis-step off the obliterated sidewalk and sank up to her knees in a snow-drift.

"Take care, Mrs. Rosen," she kept calling, "keep to the right! Don't spoil your nice coat. My, ain't this real winter? We never had it like this back with us."

When they reached the Templeton's gate, Victoria wouldn't hear of Mrs. Rosen's going farther. "No, indeed, Mrs. Rosen, you come right in with me and get dry, and Ma'll make you a hot toddy while I take the baby."

By this time Mrs. Rosen had begun to like her neighbour, so she went in. To her surprise, the parlour was neat and comfortable — the children did not strew things about there, apparently. The hard-coal burner threw out a warm red glow. A faded, respectable Brussels carpet covered the floor, an old-fashioned wooden clock ticked on the walnut bookcase. There were a few easy chairs, and no hideous ornaments about. She rather liked the old oil-chromos on the wall: " Hagar and Ishmael in the Wilderness," and " The Light of the World." While Mrs. Rosen dried her feet on the nickel base of the stove, Mrs. Templeton excused herself and withdrew to the next room, — her bedroom, — took off her silk dress and corsets, and put on a white challis négligée. She reappeared with the baby, who was not crying, exactly, but making eager, passionate, gasping entreaties, — faster and faster, tenser and tenser, as he felt his dinner nearer and nearer and yet not his.

Mrs. Templeton sat down in a low rocker by the stove and began to nurse him, holding him snugly but carelessly, still talking to Mrs. Rosen about the card party, and laughing about their wade home through the snow. Hughie, the baby, fell to work so fiercely that beads of sweat came out all over his flushed forehead. Mrs. Rosen could not help admiring him and his mother. They were so comfortable and complete. When he was changed to the other side, Hughie resented the interruption a little; but after a time he became soft and bland, as smooth as oil, indeed; began looking about him as he drew in his milk. He finally dropped the nipple from his lips altogether, turned on his mother's arm, and looked inquiringly at Mrs. Rosen.

"What a beautiful baby!" she exclaimed from her heart. And he was. A sort of golden baby. His hair was like sunshine, and his long lashes were gold over such gay blue eyes. There seemed to be a gold glow in his soft pink skin, and he had the smile of a cherub.

"We think he's a pretty boy," said Mrs. Templeton. " He's the prettiest of my babies. Though the twins were mighty cunning little fellows. I hated the idea of twins, but the minute I saw them, I couldn't resist them."

Just then old Mrs. Harris came in, walking widely in her full-gathered skirt and felt-soled shoes, bearing a tray with two smoking goblets upon it.

"This is my mother, Mrs. Harris, Mrs. Rosen," said Mrs. Templeton.

"I'm glad to know you, ma'am," said Mrs. Harris. "Victoria, let me take the baby, while you two ladies have your toddy."

"Oh, don't take him away, Mrs. Harris, please!" cried Mrs. Rosen.

The old lady smiled. "I won't. I'll set right here. He never frets with his grandma."

When Mrs. Rosen had finished her excellent drink, she asked if she might hold the baby, and Mrs. Harris placed him on her lap. He made a few rapid boxing motions with his two fists, then braced himself on his heels and the back of his head, and lifted himself up in an arc. When he dropped back, he looked up at Mrs. Rosen with his most intimate smile. "See what a smart boy I am!"

When Mrs. Rosen walked home, feeling her way through the snow by following the fence, she knew she could never stay away from a house where there was a baby like that one.

IV

Vickie did her studying in a hammock hung
between two tall cottonwood trees over in the
Roadmaster's green yard. The Roadmaster
had the finest yard in Skyline, on the edge of
the town, just where the sandy plain and the
sage-brush began. His family went back to
Ohio every summer, and Bert and Del Templeton were paid to take care of his lawn, to
turn the sprinkler on at the right hours and to
cut the grass. They were really too little to run
the heavy lawn-mower very well, but they were
able to manage because they were twins. Each
took one end of the handle-bar, and they
pushed together like a pair of fat Shetland
ponies. They were very proud of being able to
keep the lawn so nice, and worked hard on it.
They cut Mrs. Rosen's grass once a week, too,
and did it so well that she wondered why in the
world they never did anything about their own
yard. They didn't have city water, to be sure
(it was expensive), but she thought they might
pick up a few velocipedes and iron hoops, and

dig up the messy " flower-bed," that was even uglier than the naked gravel spots. She was particularly offended by a deep ragged ditch, a miniature arroyo, which ran across the back yard, serving no purpose and looking very dreary.

One morning she said craftily to the twins, when she was paying them for cutting her grass:

" And, boys, why don't you just shovel the sand-pile by your fence into dat ditch, and make your back yard smooth? "

" Oh, no, ma'am," said Adelbert with feeling. " We like to have the ditch to build bridges over! "

Ever since vacation began, the twins had been busy getting the Roadmaster's yard ready for the Methodist lawn party. When Mrs. Holliday, the Roadmaster's wife, went away for the summer, she always left a key with the Ladies' Aid Society and invited them to give their ice-cream social at her place.

This year the date set for the party was June fifteenth. The day was a particularly fine one, and as Mr. Holliday himself had been called to Cheyenne on railroad business, the twins felt personally responsible for everything. They got out to the Holliday place early in the morning, and stayed on guard all day. Before noon the drayman brought a wagon-load of card-tables and folding chairs, which the boys placed in chosen spots under the cottonwood trees. In the afternoon the Methodist ladies arrived and opened up the kitchen to receive the freezers of home-made ice-cream, and the cakes which the congregation donated. Indeed, all the good cake-bakers in town were expected to send a cake. Grandma Harris baked a white cake, thickly iced and covered with freshly grated coconut, and Vickie took it over in the afternoon.

Mr. and Mrs. Rosen, because they belonged to no church, contributed to the support of all, and usually went to the church suppers in winter and the socials in summer. On this warm June evening they set out early, in order to take a walk first. They strolled along the hard gravelled road that led out through the sage to-

ward the sand-hills; tonight it led toward the
moon, just rising over the sweep of dunes.
The sky was almost as blue as at midday, and
had that look of being very near and very soft
which it has in desert countries. The moon, too,
looked very near, soft and bland and innocent.
Mrs. Rosen admitted that in the Adirondacks,
for which she was always secretly homesick
in summer, the moon had a much colder bril-
liance, seemed farther off and made of a harder
metal. This moon gave the sage-brush plain
and the drifted sand-hills the softness of velvet.
All countries were beautiful to Mr. Rosen. He
carried a country of his own in his mind,
and was able to unfold it like a tent in any
wilderness.

When they at last turned back toward the
town, they saw groups of people, women in
white dresses, walking toward the dark spot
where the paper lanterns made a yellow light
underneath the cottonwoods. High above, the
rustling tree-tops stirred free in the flood of
moonlight.

The lighted yard was surrounded by a low

board fence, painted the dark red Burlington
colour, and as the Rosens drew near, they noticed four children standing close together in
the shadow of some tall elder bushes just outside the fence. They were the poor Maude
children; their mother was the washwoman,
the Rosens' laundress and the Templetons'.
People said that every one of those children
had a different father. But good laundresses
were few, and even the members of the Ladies'
Aid were glad to get Mrs. Maude's services at
a dollar a day, though they didn't like their
children to play with hers. Just as the Rosens
approached, Mrs. Templeton came out from
the lighted square, leaned over the fence, and
addressed the little Maudes.

"I expect you children forgot your dimes,
now didn't you? Never mind, here's a dime for
each of you, so come along and have your ice-
cream."

The Maudes put out small hands and said:
"Thank you," but not one of them moved.

"Come along, Francie" (the oldest girl
was named Frances). "Climb right over the

fence." Mrs. Templeton reached over and gave
her a hand, and the little boys quickly scram-
bled after their sister. Mrs. Templeton took
them to a table which Vickie and the twins
had just selected as being especially private —
they liked to do things together.

"Here, Vickie, let the Maudes sit at your
table, and take care they get plenty of cake."

The Rosens had followed close behind Mrs.
Templeton, and Mr. Rosen now overtook her
and said in his most courteous and friendly
manner: "Good evening, Mrs. Templeton.
Will you have ice-cream with us?" He always
used the local idioms, though his voice and
enunciation made them sound altogether different from Skyline speech.

"Indeed I will, Mr. Rosen. Mr. Templeton will be late. He went out to his farm
yesterday, and I don't know just when to expect him."

Vickie and the twins were disappointed at
not having their table to themselves, when they
had come early and found a nice one; but they
knew it was right to look out for the dreary

little Maudes, so they moved close together and
made room for them. The Maudes didn't
cramp them long. When the three boys had
eaten the last crumb of cake and licked their
spoons, Francie got up and led them to a green
slope by the fence, just outside the lighted circle. " Now set down, and watch and see how
folks do," she told them. The boys looked to
Francie for commands and support. She was
really Amos Maude's child, born before he
ran away to the Klondike, and it had been
rubbed into them that this made a difference.

The Templeton children made their ice-
cream linger out, and sat watching the crowd.
They were glad to see their mother go to Mr.
Rosen's table, and noticed how nicely he placed
a chair for her and insisted upon putting a
scarf about her shoulders. Their mother was
wearing her new dotted Swiss, with many ruf-
fles, all edged with black ribbon, and wide
ruffly sleeves. As the twins watched her over
their spoons, they thought how much prettier
their mother was than any of the other women,
and how becoming her new dress was. The

children got as much satisfaction as Mrs. Harris out of Victoria's good looks.

Mr. Rosen was well pleased with Mrs. Templeton and her new dress, and with her kindness to the little Maudes. He thought her manner with them just right, — warm, spontaneous, without anything patronizing. He always admired her way with her own children, though Mrs. Rosen thought it too casual. Being a good mother, he believed, was much more a matter of physical poise and richness than of sentimentalizing and reading doctor-books. Tonight he was more talkative than usual, and in his quiet way made Mrs. Templeton feel his real friendliness and admiration. Unfortunately, he made other people feel it, too.

Mrs. Jackson, a neighbour who didn't like the Templetons, had been keeping an eye on Mr. Rosen's table. She was a stout square woman of imperturbable calm, effective in regulating the affairs of the community because she never lost her temper, and could say the most cutting things in calm, even kindly, tones. Her face was smooth and placid as a mask, rather good-humoured, and the fact that one eye had a cast and looked askance made it the more difficult to see through her intentions. When she had been lingering about the Rosens' table for some time, studying Mr. Rosen's pleasant attentions to Mrs. Templeton, she brought up a trayful of cake.

"You folks are about ready for another helping," she remarked affably.

Mrs. Rosen spoke. "I want some of Grandma Harris's cake. It's a white coconut, Mrs. Jackson."

"How about you, Mrs. Templeton, would you like some of your own cake?"

"Indeed I would," said Mrs. Templeton heartily. "Ma said she had good luck with it. I didn't see it. Vickie brought it over."

Mrs. Jackson deliberately separated the slices on her tray with two forks. "Well," she remarked with a chuckle that really sounded amiable, "I don't know but I'd like my cakes, if I kept somebody in the kitchen to bake them for me."

Mr. Rosen for once spoke quickly. "If I

had a cook like Grandma Harris in my kitchen, I'd live in it!" he declared.

Mrs. Jackson smiled. "I don't know as we feel like that, Mrs. Templeton? I tell Mr. Jackson that my idea of coming up in the world would be to forget I had a cook-stove, like Mrs. Templeton. But we can't all be lucky."

Mr. Rosen could not tell how much was malice and how much was stupidity. What he chiefly detected was self-satisfaction; the craftiness of the coarse-fibred country girl putting catch questions to the teacher. Yes, he decided, the woman was merely showing off, — she regarded it as an accomplishment to make people uncomfortable.

Mrs. Templeton didn't at once take it in. Her training was all to the end that you must give a guest everything you have, even if he happens to be your worst enemy, and that to cause anyone embarrassment is a frightful and humiliating blunder. She felt hurt without knowing just why, but all evening it kept growing clearer to her that this was another of those thrusts from the outside which she couldn't understand. The neighbours were sure to take sides against her, apparently, if they came often to see her mother.

Mr. Rosen tried to distract Mrs. Templeton, but he could feel the poison working. On the way home the children knew something had displeased or hurt their mother. When they went into the house, she told them to go upstairs at once, as she had a headache. She was severe and distant. When Mrs. Harris suggested making her some peppermint tea, Victoria threw up her chin.

"I don't want anybody waiting on me. I just want to be let alone." And she withdrew without saying good-night, or "Are you all right, Ma?" as she usually did.

Left alone, Mrs. Harris sighed and began to turn down her bed. She knew, as well as if she had been at the social, what kind of thing had happened. Some of those prying ladies of the Woman's Relief Corps, or the Woman's Christian Temperance Union, had been intimating to Victoria that her mother was "put upon." Nothing ever made Victoria cross but criticism. She was jealous of small attentions paid to Mrs. Harris, because she felt they were paid " behind her back " or " over her head," in a way that implied reproach to her. Victoria had been a belle in their own town in Tennessee, but here she was not very popular, no matter how many pretty dresses she wore, and she couldn't bear it. She felt as if her mother and Mr. Templeton must be somehow to blame; at least they ought to protect her from whatever was disagreeable — they always had!

v

Mrs. Harris wakened at about four o'clock, as usual, before the house was stirring, and lay thinking about their position in this new town. She didn't know why the neighbours acted so; she was as much in the dark as Victoria. At home, back in Tennessee, her place in the family was not exceptional, but perfectly regular. Mrs. Harris had replied to Mrs. Rosen, when that lady asked why in the world she didn't break Vickie in to help her in the kitchen: "We are only young once, and trouble comes soon enough." Young girls, in the South, were supposed to be carefree and foolish; the fault Grandmother found in Vickie was that she wasn't foolish enough. When the foolish girl married and began to have children, everything else must give way to that. She must be humoured and given the best of everything, because having children was hard on a woman, and it was the most important thing in the world. In Tennessee every young married woman in good circumstances had an older woman in the house, a mother or mother-in-law or an old aunt, who managed the household economies and directed the help.

That was the great difference; in Tennessee there had been plenty of helpers. There was old Miss Sadie Crummer, who came to the house to spin and sew and mend; old Mrs. Smith, who always arrived to help at butchering- and preserving-time; Lizzie, the coloured girl, who did the washing and who ran in every day to help Mandy. There were plenty more, who came whenever one of Lizzie's barefoot boys ran to fetch them. The hills were full of solitary old women, or women but slightly attached to some household, who were glad to come to Miz' Harris's for good food and a warm bed, and the little present that either Mrs. Harris or Victoria slipped into their carpet-sack when they went away.

To be sure, Mrs. Harris, and the other women of her age who managed their daughter's house, kept in the background; but it was their own background, and they ruled it jealously. They left the front porch and the parlour to the young married couple and their young friends; the old women spent most of their lives in the kitchen and pantries and back dining-room. But there they ordered life to their own taste, entertained their friends, dispensed charity, and heard the troubles of the poor. Moreover, back there it was Grandmother's own house they lived in. Mr. Templeton came of a superior family and had what

Grandmother called "blood," but no property. He never so much as mended one of the steps to the front porch without consulting Mrs. Harris. Even "back home," in the aristocracy, there were old women who went on living like young ones, — gave parties and drove out in their carriage and "went North" in the summer. But among the middle-class people and the country-folk, when a woman was a widow and had married daughters, she considered herself an old woman and wore full-gathered black dresses and a black bonnet and became a housekeeper. She accepted this estate unprotestingly, almost gratefully.

The Templetons' troubles began when Mr. Templeton's aunt died and left him a few thousand dollars, and he got the idea of bettering himself. The twins were little then, and he told Mrs. Harris his boys would have a better chance in Colorado — everybody was going West. He went alone first, and got a good position with a mining company in the mountains of southern Colorado. He had been book-keeper in the bank in his home town, had

" grown up in the bank," as they said. He was industrious and honourable, and the managers of the mining company liked him, even if they laughed at his polite, soft-spoken manners. He could have held his position indefinitely, and maybe got a promotion. But the altitude of that mountain town was too high for his family. All the children were sick there; Mrs. Templeton was ill most of the time and nearly died when Ronald was born. Hillary Templeton lost his courage and came north to the flat, sunny, semi-arid country between Wray and Cheyenne, to work for an irrigation project. So far, things had not gone well with him. The pinch told on everyone, but most on Grandmother. Here, in Skyline, she had all her accustomed responsibilities, and no helper but Mandy. Mrs. Harris was no longer living in a feudal society, where there were plenty of landless people glad to render service to the more fortunate, but in a snappy little Western democracy, where every man was as good as his neighbour and out to prove it.

Neither Mrs. Harris nor Mrs. Templeton

understood just what was the matter; they were hurt and dazed, merely. Victoria knew that here she was censured and criticized, she who had always been so admired and envied! Grandmother knew that these meddlesome "Northerners" said things that made Victoria suspicious and unlike herself; made her unwilling that Mrs. Harris should receive visitors alone, or accept marks of attention that seemed offered in compassion for her state.

These women who belonged to clubs and Relief Corps lived differently, Mrs. Harris knew, but she herself didn't like the way they lived. She believed that somebody ought to be in the parlour, and somebody in the kitchen. She wouldn't for the world have had Victoria go about every morning in a short gingham dress, with bare arms, and a dust-cap on her head to hide the curling-kids, as these brisk housekeepers did. To Mrs. Harris that would have meant real poverty, coming down in the world so far that one could no longer keep up appearances. Her life was hard now, to be sure, since the family went on increasing and

Mr. Templeton's means went on decreasing; but she certainly valued respectability above personal comfort, and she could go on a good way yet if they always had a cool pleasant parlour, with Victoria properly dressed to receive visitors. To keep Victoria different from these "ordinary" women meant everything to Mrs. Harris. She realized that Mrs. Rosen managed to be mistress of any situation, either in kitchen or parlour, but that was because she was "foreign." Grandmother perfectly understood that their neighbour had a superior cultivation which made everything she did an exercise of skill. She knew well enough that their own ways of cooking and cleaning were primitive beside Mrs. Rosen's.

If only Mr. Templeton's business affairs would look up, they could rent a larger house, and everything would be better. They might even get a German girl to come in and help, — but now there was no place to put her. Grandmother's own lot could improve only with the family fortunes — any comfort for herself, aside from that of the family, was inconceivable to her; and on the other hand she could have no real unhappiness while the children were well, and good, and fond of her and their mother. That was why it was worth while to get up early in the morning and make her bed neat and draw the red spread smooth. The little boys loved to lie on her lounge and her pillows when they were tired. When they were sick, Ronald and Hughie wanted to be in her lap. They had no physical shrinking from her because she was old. And Victoria was never jealous of the children's wanting to be with her so much; that was a mercy!

Sometimes, in the morning, if her feet ached more than usual, Mrs. Harris felt a little low. (Nobody did anything about broken arches in those days, and the common endurance test of old age was to keep going after every step cost something.) She would hang up her towel with a sigh and go into the kitchen, feeling that it was hard to make a start. But the moment she heard the children running down the uncarpeted back stairs, she forgot to be low. Indeed, she ceased to be an individual, an old woman with aching feet; she became part of a group, became a relationship. She was drunk up into their freshness when they burst in upon her, telling her about their dreams, explaining their troubles with buttons and shoe-laces and underwear shrunk too small. The tired, solitary old woman Grandmother had been at daybreak vanished; suddenly the morning seemed as important to her as it did to the children, and the mornings ahead stretched out sunshiny, important.

VI

The day after the Methodist social, Blue Boy didn't come for his morning milk; he always had it in a clean saucer on the covered back porch, under the long bench where the tin wash-tubs stood ready for Mrs. Maude. After the children had finished breakfast, Mrs. Harris sent Mandy out to look for the cat.

The girl came back in a minute, her eyes big.

"Law me, Miz' Harris, he's awful sick. He's a-layin' in the straw in the barn. He's swallered a bone, or havin' a fit or somethin'."

Grandmother threw an apron over her head and went out to see for herself. The children went with her. Blue Boy was retching and choking, and his yellow eyes were filled up with rhume.

"Oh, Gram'ma, what's the matter?" the boys cried.

"It's the distemper. How could he have got it?" Her voice was so harsh that Ronald began to cry. "Take Ronald back to the house, Del. He might get bit. I wish I'd kept my word and never had a cat again!"

"Why, Gram'ma!" Albert looked at her. "Won't Blue Boy get well?"

"Not from the distemper, he won't."

"But Gram'ma, can't I run for the veter'nary?"

"You gether up an armful of hay. We'll take him into the coal-house, where I can watch him."

Mrs. Harris waited until the spasm was

over, then picked up the limp cat and carried him to the coal-shed that opened off the back porch. Albert piled the hay in one corner — the coal was low, since it was summer — and they spread a piece of old carpet on the hay and made a bed for Blue Boy. " Now you run along with Adelbert. There'll be a lot of work to do on Mr. Holliday's yard, cleaning up after the sociable. Mandy an' me'll watch Blue Boy. I expect he'll sleep for a while."

Albert went away regretfully, but the dray-man and some of the Methodist ladies were in Mr. Holliday's yard, packing chairs and tables and ice-cream freezers into the wagon, and the twins forgot the sick cat in their excitement. By noon they had picked up the last paper napkin, raked over the gravel walks where the salt from the freezers had left white patches, and hung the hammock in which Vickie did her studying back in its place. Mr. Holliday paid the boys a dollar a week for keeping up the yard, and they gave the money to their mother — it didn't come amiss in a family where actual cash was so short. She let

them keep half the sum Mrs. Rosen paid for her
milk every Saturday, and that was more spend-
ing money than most boys had. They often
made a few extra quarters by cutting grass for
other people, or by distributing handbills. Even
the disagreeable Mrs. Jackson next door had
remarked over the fence to Mrs. Harris: " I do
believe Bert and Del are going to be industrious. They must have got it from you,
Grandma."

The day came on very hot, and when the
twins got back from the Roadmaster's yard,
they both lay down on Grandmother's lounge
and went to sleep. After dinner they had a
rare opportunity; the Roadmaster himself
appeared at the front door and invited them
to go up to the next town with him on his railroad velocipede. That was great fun: the
velocipede always whizzed along so fast on
the bright rails, the gasoline engine puffing;
and grasshoppers jumped up out of the sage-
brush and hit you in the face like sling-shot bul-
lets. Sometimes the wheels cut in two a lazy
snake who was sunning himself on the track,

and the twins always hoped it was a rattler and felt they had done a good work.

The boys got back from their trip with Mr. Holliday late in the afternoon. The house was cool and quiet. Their mother had taken Ronald and Hughie down town with her, and Vickie was off somewhere. Grandmother was not in her room, and the kitchen was empty. The boys went out to the back porch to pump a drink. The coal-shed door was open, and inside, on a low stool, sat Mrs. Harris beside her cat. Bert and Del didn't stop to get a drink; they felt ashamed that they had gone off for a gay ride and forgotten Blue Boy. They sat down on a big lump of coal beside Mrs. Harris. They would never have known that this miserable rumpled animal was their proud tom. Presently he went off into a spasm and began to froth at the mouth.

"Oh, Gram'ma, can't you do anything?" cried Albert, struggling with his tears. "Blue Boy was such a good cat, — why has he got to suffer?"

"Everything that's alive has got to suffer,"

said Mrs. Harris. Albert put out his hand and caught her skirt, looking up at her beseechingly, as if to make her unsay that saying, which he only half understood. She patted his hand. She had forgot she was speaking to a little boy.

"Where's Vickie?" Adelbert asked aggrievedly. "Why don't she do something? He's part her cat."

Mrs. Harris sighed. "Vickie's got her head full of things lately; that makes people kind of heartless."

The boys resolved they would never put anything into their heads, then!

Blue Boy's fit passed, and the three sat watching their pet that no longer knew them. The twins had not seen much suffering; Grandmother had seen a great deal. Back in Tennessee, in her own neighbourhood, she was accounted a famous nurse. When any of the poor mountain people were in great distress, they always sent for Miz' Harris. Many a time she had gone into a house where five or six children were all down with scarlet fever or diphtheria, and done what she could. Many a child and many a woman she had laid out and got ready for the grave. In her primitive community the undertaker made the coffin, — he did nothing more. She had seen so much misery that she wondered herself why it hurt so to see her tom-cat die. She had taken her leave of him, and she got up from her stool. She didn't want the boys to be too much distressed.

" Now you boys must wash and put on clean shirts. Your mother will be home pretty soon. We'll leave Blue Boy; he'll likely be easier in the morning." She knew the cat would die at sundown.

After supper, when Bert looked into the coal-shed and found the cat dead, all the family were sad. Ronald cried miserably, and Hughie cried because Ronald did. Mrs. Templeton herself went out and looked into the shed, and she was sorry, too. Though she didn't like cats, she had been fond of this one.

" Hillary," she told her husband, " when you go down town tonight, tell the Mexican to come and get that cat early in the morning, before the children are up."

The Mexican had a cart and two mules, and he hauled away tin cans and refuse to a gully out in the sage-brush.

Mrs. Harris gave Victoria an indignant glance when she heard this, and turned back to the kitchen. All evening she was gloomy and silent. She refused to read aloud, and the twins took Ronald and went mournfully out to play under the electric light. Later, when they had said good-night to their parents in the parlour and were on their way upstairs, Mrs. Harris followed them into the kitchen, shut the door behind her, and said indignantly:

"Air you two boys going to let that Mexican take Blue Boy and throw him onto some trash-pile?"

The sleepy boys were frightened at the anger and bitterness in her tone. They stood still and looked up at her, while she went on:

"You git up early in the morning, and I'll put him in a sack, and one of you take a spade and go to that crooked old willer tree that grows just where the sand creek turns off the road, and you dig a little grave for Blue Boy, an' bury him right."

They had seldom seen such resentment in their grandmother. Albert's throat choked up, he rubbed the tears away with his fist.

"Yes'm, Gram'ma, we will, we will," he gulped.

VII

Only Mrs. Harris saw the boys go out next morning. She slipped a bread-and-butter sandwich into the hand of each, but she said nothing, and they said nothing.

The boys did not get home until their parents were ready to leave the table. Mrs. Templeton made no fuss, but told them to sit down and eat their breakfast. When they had finished, she said commandingly:

"Now you march into my room." That was where she heard explanations and administered punishment. When she whipped them, she did it thoroughly.

She followed them and shut the door.

"Now, what were you boys doing this morning?"

"We went off to bury Blue Boy."

"Why didn't you tell me you were going?"

They looked down at their toes, but said nothing. Their mother studied their mournful faces, and her overbearing expression softened.

"The next time you get up and go off anywhere, you come and tell me beforehand, do you understand?"

"Yes'm."

She opened the door, motioned them out, and went with them into the parlour. "I'm sorry about your cat, boys," she said. "That's why I don't like to have cats around; they're always getting sick and dying. Now run along and play. Maybe you'd like to have a circus in the back yard this afternoon? And we'll all come."

The twins ran out in a joyful frame of mind.

Their grandmother had been mistaken; their mother wasn't indifferent about Blue Boy, she was sorry. Now everything was all right, and they could make a circus ring.

They knew their grandmother got put out about strange things, anyhow. A few months ago it was because their mother hadn't asked one of the visiting preachers who came to the church conference to stay with them. There was no place for the preacher to sleep except on the folding lounge in the parlour, and no place for him to wash — he would have been very uncomfortable, and so would all the household. But Mrs. Harris was terribly upset that there should be a conference in the town, and they not keeping a preacher! She was quite bitter about it.

The twins called in the neighbour boys, and they made a ring in the back yard, around their turning-bar. Their mother came to the show and paid admission, bringing Mrs. Rosen and Grandma Harris. Mrs. Rosen thought if all the children in the neighbourhood were to be howling and running in a circle in the

Templetons' back yard, she might as well be there, too, for she would have no peace at home.

After the dog races and the Indian fight were over, Mrs. Templeton took Mrs. Rosen into the house to revive her with cake and lemonade. The parlour was cool and dusky. Mrs. Rosen was glad to get into it after sitting on a wooden bench in the sun. Grandmother stayed in the parlour with them, which was unusual. Mrs. Rosen sat waving a palm-leaf fan, — she felt the heat very much, because she wore her stays so tight — while Victoria went to make the lemonade.

"De circuses are not so good, widout Vickie to manage them, Grandma," she said.

"No'm. The boys complain right smart about losing Vickie from their plays. She's at her books all the time now. I don't know what's got into the child."

"If she wants to go to college, she must prepare herself, Grandma. I am agreeably surprised in her. I didn't think she'd stick to it."

Mrs. Templeton came in with a tray of tum-

blers and the glass pitcher all frosted over.
Mrs. Rosen wistfully admired her neighbour's
tall figure and good carriage; she was wearing
no corsets at all today under her flowered or-
gandie afternoon dress, Mrs. Rosen had noticed, and yet she could carry herself so smooth
and straight, — after having had so many children, too! Mrs. Rosen was envious, but she
gave credit where credit was due.

When Mrs. Templeton brought in the cake,
Mrs. Rosen was still talking to Grandmother
about Vickie's studying. Mrs. Templeton
shrugged carelessly.

" There's such a thing as overdoing it, Mrs.
Rosen," she observed as she poured the lemonade. " Vickie's very apt to run to extremes."

" But, my dear lady, she can hardly be too
extreme in dis matter. If she is to take a com-
petitive examination with girls from much
better schools than ours, she will have to do
better than the others, or fail; no two ways
about it. We must encourage her."

Mrs. Templeton bridled a little. " I'm sure
I don't interfere with her studying, Mrs.

Rosen. I don't see where she got this notion, but I let her alone."

Mrs. Rosen accepted a second piece of chocolate cake. "And what do you think about it, Grandma?"

Mrs. Harris smiled politely. "None of our people, or Mr. Templeton's either, ever went to college. I expect it is all on account of the young gentleman who was here last summer."

Mrs. Rosen laughed and lifted her eyebrows. "Something very personal in Vickie's admiration for Professor Chalmers we think, Grandma? A very sudden interest in de sciences, I should say!"

Mrs. Templeton shrugged. "You're mistaken, Mrs. Rosen. There ain't a particle of romance in Vickie."

"But there are several kinds of romance, Mrs. Templeton. She may not have your kind."

"Yes'm, that's so," said Mrs. Harris in a low, grateful voice. She thought that a hard word Victoria had said of Vickie.

"I didn't see a thing in that Professor

Chalmers, myself," Victoria remarked. "He was a gawky kind of fellow, and never had a thing to say in company. Did you think he amounted to much?"

"Oh, widout doubt Doctor Chalmers is a very scholarly man. A great many brilliant scholars are widout de social graces, you know." When Mrs. Rosen, from a much wider experience, corrected her neighbour, she did so somewhat playfully, as if insisting upon something Victoria capriciously chose to ignore.

At this point old Mrs. Harris put her hands on the arms of the chair in preparation to rise. "If you ladies will excuse me, I think I will go and lie down a little before supper." She rose and went heavily out on her felt soles. She never really lay down in the afternoon, but she dozed in her own black rocker. Mrs. Rosen and Victoria sat chatting about Professor Chalmers and his boys.

Last summer the young professor had come to Skyline with four of his students from the University of Michigan, and had stayed three months, digging for fossils out in the sand-hills. Vickie had spent a great many mornings at their camp. They lived at the town hotel, and drove out to their camp every day in a light spring-wagon. Vickie used to wait for them at the edge of the town, in front of the Road-master's house, and when the spring-wagon came rattling along, the boys would call: "There's our girl!" slow the horses, and give her a hand up. They said she was their mascot, and were very jolly with her. They had a splendid summer, — found a great bed of fossil elephant bones, where a whole herd must once have perished. Later on they came upon the bones of a new kind of elephant, scarcely larger than a pig. They were greatly excited about their finds, and so was Vickie. That was why they liked her. It was they who told her about a memorial scholarship at Ann Arbor, which was open to any girl from Colorado.

VIII

In August Vickie went down to Denver to take her examinations. Mr. Holliday, the Roadmaster, got her a pass, and arranged that she should stay with the family of one of his passenger conductors.

For three days she wrote examination papers along with other contestants, in one of the Denver high schools, proctored by a teacher. Her father had given her five dollars for incidental expenses, and she came home with a box of mineral specimens for the twins, a singing top for Ronald, and a toy burro for Hughie.

Then began days of suspense that stretched into weeks. Vickie went to the post-office every morning, opened her father's combination box, and looked over the letters, long before he got down town, — always hoping there might be a letter from Ann Arbor. The night mail came in at six, and after supper she hurried to the post-office and waited about until the shutter at the general-delivery window was drawn back, a signal that the mail had all been " distributed." While the tedious process of distribution was going on, she usually withdrew from the office, full of joking men and cigar smoke, and walked up and down under the big cottonwood trees that overhung the side street. When the crowd of men began to come out, then she knew the mail-bags were empty, and she went in to get whatever letters were in the Templeton box and take them home.

After two weeks went by, she grew downhearted. Her young professor, she knew, was in England for his vacation. There would be no one at the University of Michigan who was interested in her fate. Perhaps the fortunate contestant had already been notified of her success. She never asked herself, as she walked up and down under the cottonwoods on those summer nights, what she would do if she didn't get the scholarship. There was no alternative. If she didn't get it, then everything was over.

During the weeks when she lived only to go to the post-office, she managed to cut her finger

and get ink into the cut. As a result, she had a
badly infected hand and had to carry it in a
sling. When she walked her nightly beat under
the cottonwoods, it was a kind of comfort to
feel that finger throb; it was companionship,
made her case more complete.

The strange thing was that one morning a
letter came, addressed to Miss Victoria Templeton; in a long envelope such as her father
called "legal size," with *"University of
Michigan"* in the upper left-hand corner.
When Vickie took it from the box, such a wave
of fright and weakness went through her that
she could scarcely get out of the post-office.
She hid the letter under her striped blazer and
went a weak, uncertain trail down the sidewalk
under the big trees. Without seeing anything
or knowing what road she took, she got to the
Roadmaster's green yard and her hammock,
where she always felt not on the earth, yet of it.

Three hours later, when Mrs. Rosen was
just tasting one of those clear soups upon
which the Templetons thought she wasted so

much pains and good meat, Vickie walked in
at the kitchen door and said in a low but somewhat unnatural voice:

"Mrs. Rosen, I got the scholarship."

Mrs. Rosen looked up at her sharply, then
pushed the soup back to a cooler part of the
stove.

"What is dis you say, Vickie? You have
heard from de University?"

"Yes'm. I got the letter this morning." She
produced it from under her blazer.

Mrs. Rosen had been cutting noodles. She
took Vickie's face in two hot, plump hands
that were still floury, and looked at her intently. "Is dat true, Vickie? No mistake? I am
delighted — and surprised! Yes, surprised.
Den you will *be* something, you won't just sit
on de front porch." She squeezed the girl's
round, good-natured cheeks, as if she could
mould them into something definite then and
there. "Now you must stay for lunch and tell
us all about it. Go in and announce yourself to
Mr. Rosen."

Mr. Rosen had come home for lunch and

was sitting, a book in his hand, in a corner of the darkened front parlour where a flood of yellow sun streamed in under the dark green blind. He smiled his friendly smile at Vickie and waved her to a seat, making her understand that he wanted to finish his paragraph. The dark engraving of the pointed cypresses and the Roman tomb was on the wall just behind him.

Mrs. Rosen came into the back parlour, which was the dining-room, and began taking things out of the silver-drawer to lay a place for their visitor. She spoke to her husband rapidly in German.

He put down his book, came over, and took Vickie's hand.

" Is it true, Vickie? Did you really win the scholarship? "

" Yes, sir."

He stood looking down at her through his kind, remote smile, — a smile in the eyes, that seemed to come up through layers and layers of something — gentle doubts, kindly reservations.

"Why do you want to go to college, Vickie?" he asked playfully.

"To learn," she said with surprise.

"But why do you want to learn? What do you want to do with it?"

"I don't know. Nothing, I guess."

"Then what do you want it for?"

"I don't know. I just want it."

For some reason Vickie's voice broke there. She had been terribly strung up all morning, lying in the hammock with her eyes tight shut. She had not been home at all, she had wanted to take her letter to the Rosens first. And now one of the gentlest men she knew made her choke by something strange and presageful in his voice.

"Then if you want it without any purpose at all, you will not be disappointed." Mr. Rosen wished to distract her and help her to keep back the tears. "Listen: a great man once said: '*Le but n'est rien; le chemin, c'est tout.*' That means: The end is nothing, the road is all. Let me write it down for you and give you your first French lesson."

He went to the desk with its big silver ink-well, where he and his wife wrote so many letters in several languages, and inscribed the sentence on a sheet of purple paper, in his delicately shaded foreign script, signing under it a name: *J. Michelet*. He brought it back and shook it before Vickie's eyes. " There, keep it to remember me by. Slip it into the envelope with your college credentials, — that is a good place for it." From his deliberate smile and the twitch of one eyebrow, Vickie knew he meant her to take it along as an antidote, a corrective for whatever colleges might do to her. But she had always known that Mr. Rosen was wiser than professors.

Mrs. Rosen was frowning, she thought that sentence a bad precept to give any Templeton. Moreover, she always promptly called her husband back to earth when he soared a little; though it was exactly for this transcendental quality of mind that she reverenced him in her heart, and thought him so much finer than any of his successful brothers.

"Luncheon is served," she said in the crisp

tone that put people in their places. "And Miss Vickie, you are to eat your tomatoes with an oil dressing, as we do. If you are going off into the world, it is quite time you learn to like things that are everywhere accepted."

Vickie said: "Yes'm," and slipped into the chair Mr. Rosen had placed for her. Today she didn't care what she ate, though ordinarily she thought a French dressing tasted a good deal like castor oil.

IX

Vickie was to discover that nothing comes easily in this world. Next day she got a letter from one of the jolly students of Professor Chalmers's party, who was watching over her case in his chief's absence. He told her the scholarship meant admission to the freshman class without further examinations, and two hundred dollars toward her expenses; she would have to bring along about three hundred more to put her through the year.

She took this letter to her father's office. Seated in his revolving desk-chair, Mr. Templeton read it over several times and looked embarrassed.

"I'm sorry, daughter," he said at last, "but really, just now, I couldn't spare that much. Not this year. I expect next year will be better for us."

"But the scholarship is for this year, Father. It wouldn't count next year. I just have to go in September."

"I really ain't got it, daughter." He spoke, oh so kindly! He had lovely manners with his daughter and his wife. "It's just all I can do to keep the store bills paid up. I'm away behind with Mr. Rosen's bill. Couldn't you study here this winter and get along about as fast? It isn't that I wouldn't like to let you have the money if I had it. And with young children, I can't let my life insurance go."

Vickie didn't say anything more. She took her letter and wandered down Main Street with it, leaving young Mr. Templeton to a very bad half-hour.

At dinner Vickie was silent, but everyone could see she had been crying. Mr. Templeton told *Uncle Remus* stories to keep up the family morale and make the giggly twins laugh. Mrs. Templeton glanced covertly at her daughter from time to time. She was sometimes a little afraid of Vickie, who seemed to her to have a hard streak. If it were a love-affair that the girl was crying about, that would be so much more natural — and more hopeful!

At two o'clock Mrs. Templeton went to the Afternoon Euchre Club, the twins were to have another ride with the Roadmaster on his velocipede, the little boys took their nap on their mother's bed. The house was empty and quiet. Vickie felt an aversion for the hammock under the cottonwoods where she had been betrayed into such bright hopes. She lay down on her grandmother's lounge in the cluttered play-room and turned her face to the wall.

When Mrs. Harris came in for her rest and began to wash her face at the tin basin, Vickie

got up. She wanted to be alone. Mrs. Harris
came over to her while she was still sitting on
the edge of the lounge.

" What's the matter, Vickie child? " She put
her hand on her grand-daughter's shoulder,
but Vickie shrank away. Young misery is like
that, sometimes.

" Nothing. Except that I can't go to college
after all. Papa can't let me have the money."

Mrs. Harris settled herself on the faded
cushions of her rocker. " How much is it? Tell
me about it, Vickie. Nobody's around."

Vickie told her what the conditions were,
briefly and dryly, as if she were talking to an
enemy. Everyone was an enemy; all society
was against her. She told her grandmother
the facts and then went upstairs, refusing to
be comforted.

Mrs. Harris saw her disappear through the
kitchen door, and then sat looking at the door,
her face grave, her eyes stern and sad. A poor
factory-made piece of joiner's work seldom has
to bear a look of such intense, accusing sorrow;
as if that flimsy pretence of " grained " yellow

pine were the door shut against all young aspiration.

X

Mrs. Harris had decided to speak to Mr. Templeton, but opportunities for seeing him alone were not frequent. She watched out of the kitchen window, and when she next saw him go into the barn to fork down hay for his horse, she threw an apron over her head and followed him. She waylaid him as he came down from the hayloft.

"Hillary, I want to see you about Vickie. I was wondering if you could lay hand on any of the money you got for the sale of my house back home."

Mr. Templeton was nervous. He began brushing his trousers with a little whisk-broom he kept there, hanging on a nail.

"Why, no'm, Mrs. Harris. I couldn't just conveniently call in any of it right now. You

know we had to use part of it to get moved
up here from the mines."

"I know. But I thought if there was any
left you could get at, we could let Vickie have
it. A body'd like to help the child."

"I'd like to, powerful well, Mrs. Harris. I
would, indeedy. But I'm afraid I can't manage
it right now. The fellers I've loaned to can't
pay up this year. Maybe next year — " He
was like a little boy trying to escape a
scolding, though he had never had a nagging
word from Mrs. Harris.

She looked downcast, but said nothing.

"It's all right, Mrs. Harris," he took on
his brisk business tone and hung up the brush.
"The money's perfectly safe. It's well
invested."

Invested; that was a word men always held
over women, Mrs. Harris thought, and it
always meant they could have none of their
own money. She sighed deeply.

"Well, if that's the way it is — " She turned
away and went back to the house on her flat
heelless slippers, just in time; Victoria was at

that moment coming out to the kitchen with Hughie.

"Ma," she said, "can the little boy play out here, while I go down town?"

XI

For the next few days Mrs. Harris was very sombre, and she was not well. Several times in the kitchen she was seized with what she called giddy spells, and Mandy had to help her to a chair and give her a little brandy.

"Don't you say nothin', Mandy," she warned the girl. But Mandy knew enough for that.

Mrs. Harris scarcely noticed how her strength was failing, because she had so much on her mind. She was very proud, and she wanted to do something that was hard for her to do. The difficulty was to catch Mrs. Rosen alone.

On the afternoon when Victoria went to her

weekly euchre, the old lady beckoned Mandy
and told her to run across the alley and fetch
Mrs. Rosen for a minute.

Mrs. Rosen was packing her trunk, but she
came at once. Grandmother awaited her in
her chair in the play-room.

"I take it very kindly of you to come, Mrs.
Rosen. I'm afraid it's warm in here. Won't you
have a fan?" She extended the palm leaf she
was holding.

"Keep it yourself, Grandma. You are not
looking very well. Do you feel badly, Grandma
Harris?" She took the old lady's hand and
looked at her anxiously.

"Oh, no, ma'am! I'm as well as usual. The
heat wears on me a little, maybe. Have you
seen Vickie lately, Mrs. Rosen?"

"Vickie? No. She hasn't run in for several
days. These young people are full of their own
affairs, you know."

"I expect she's backward about seeing you,
now that she's so discouraged."

"Discouraged? Why, didn't the child get
her scholarship after all?"

"Yes'm, she did. But they write her she has to bring more money to help her out; three hundred dollars. Mr. Templeton can't raise it just now. We had so much sickness in that mountain town before we moved up here, he got behind. Pore Vickie's downhearted."

"Oh, that is too bad! I expect you've been fretting over it, and that is why you don't look like yourself. Now what can we do about it?"

Mrs. Harris sighed and shook her head. "Vickie's trying to muster courage to go around to her father's friends and borrow from one and another. But we ain't been here long, —it ain't like we had old friends here. I hate to have the child do it."

Mrs. Rosen looked perplexed. "I'm sure Mr. Rosen would help her. He takes a great interest in Vickie."

"I thought maybe he could see his way to. That's why I sent Mandy to fetch you."

"That was right, Grandma. Now let me think." Mrs. Rosen put up her plump red-brown hand and leaned her chin upon it. "Day after tomorrow I am going to run on to Chicago for my niece's wedding." She saw her old friend's face fall. " Oh, I shan't be gone long; ten days, perhaps. I will speak to Mr. Rosen tonight, and if Vickie goes to him after I am off his hands, I'm sure he will help her."

Mrs. Harris looked up at her with solemn gratitude. " Vickie ain't the kind of girl would forget anything like that, Mrs. Rosen. Nor I wouldn't forget it."

Mrs. Rosen patted her arm. " Grandma Harris," she exclaimed, " I will just ask Mr. Rosen to do it for you! You know I care more about the old folks than the young. If I take this worry off your mind, I shall go away to the wedding with a light heart. Now dismiss it. I am sure Mr. Rosen can arrange this himself for you, and Vickie won't have to go about to these people here, and our gossipy neighbours will never be the wiser." Mrs. Rosen poured this out in her quick, authoritative tone, converting her *th's* into *d's,* as she did when she was excited.

Mrs. Harris's red-brown eyes slowly filled with tears, — Mrs. Rosen had never seen that happen before. But she simply said, with quiet dignity: " Thank you, ma'am. I wouldn't have turned to nobody else."

" That means I am an old friend already, doesn't it, Grandma? And that's what I want to be. I am very jealous where Grandma Harris is concerned!" She lightly kissed the back of the purple-veined hand she had been holding, and ran home to her packing. Grandma sat looking down at her hand. How easy it was for these foreigners to say what they felt!

XII

Mrs. Harris knew she was failing. She was glad to be able to conceal it from Mrs. Rosen when that kind neighbour dashed in to kiss her good-bye on the morning of her departure for Chicago. Mrs. Templeton was, of course, present, and secrets could not be discussed. Mrs. Rosen, in her stiff little brown travelling-hat, her hands tightly gloved in brown kid, could only wink and nod to Grandmother to tell her all was well. Then she went out and climbed into the " hack " bound for the depot, which had stopped for a moment at the Templetons' gate.

Mrs. Harris was thankful that her excitable friend hadn't noticed anything unusual about her looks, and, above all, that she had made no comment. She got through the day, and that evening, thank goodness, Mr. Templeton took his wife to hear a company of strolling players sing *The Chimes of Normandy* at the Opera House. He loved music, and just now he was very eager to distract and amuse Victoria. Grandma sent the twins out to play and went to bed early.

Next morning, when she joined Mandy in the kitchen, Mandy noticed something wrong.

" You set right down, Miz' Harris, an' let me git you some whisky. Deed, ma'am, you look awful porely. You ought to tell Miss Victoria an' let her send for the doctor."

" No, Mandy, I don't want no doctor. I've seen more sickness than ever he has. Doctors can't do no more than linger you out, an' I've always prayed I wouldn't last to be a burden. You git me some whisky in hot water, and pour it on a piece of toast. I feel real empty."

That afternoon when Mrs. Harris was taking her rest, for once she lay down upon her lounge. Vickie came in, tense and excited, and stopped for a moment.

"It's all right, Grandma. Mr. Rosen is going to lend me the money. I won't have to go to anybody else. He won't ask Father to endorse my note, either. He'll just take my name." Vickie rather shouted this news at Mrs. Harris, as if the old lady were deaf, or slow of understanding. She didn't thank her; she didn't know her grandmother was in any way responsible for Mr. Rosen's offer, though at the close of their interview he had said: "We won't speak of our arrangement to anyone but your father. And I want you to mention it to the old lady Harris. I know she has been worrying about you."

Having brusquely announced her news, Vickie hurried away. There was so much to do about getting ready, she didn't know where to begin. She had no trunk and no clothes. Her winter coat, bought two years ago, was so outgrown that she couldn't get into it. All her shoes were run over at the heel and must go to the cobbler. And she had only two weeks in which to do everything! She dashed off.

Mrs. Harris sighed and closed her eyes happily. She thought with modest pride that with people like the Rosens she had always " got along nicely." It was only with the ill-bred and unclassified, like this Mrs. Jackson next door, that she had disagreeable experiences. Such folks, she told herself, had come out of nothing and knew no better. She was afraid this inquisitive woman might find her ailing and come prying round with unwelcome suggestions.

Mrs. Jackson did, indeed, call that very afternoon, with a miserable contribution of veal-loaf as an excuse (all the Templetons hated veal), but Mandy had been forewarned, and she was resourceful. She met Mrs. Jackson at the kitchen door and blocked the way.

" Sh-h-h, ma'am, Miz' Harris is asleep,

havin' her nap. No'm, she ain't porely, she's as usual. But Hughie had the colic last night when Miss Victoria was at the show, an' kep' Miz' Harris awake."

Mrs. Jackson was loath to turn back. She had really come to find out why Mrs. Rosen drove away in the depot hack yesterday morning. Except at church socials, Mrs. Jackson did not meet people in Mrs. Rosen's set.

The next day, when Mrs. Harris got up and sat on the edge of her bed, her head began to swim, and she lay down again. Mandy peeped into the play-room as soon as she came downstairs, and found the old lady still in bed. She leaned over her and whispered:

"Ain't you feelin' well, Miz' Harris?"

"No, Mandy, I'm right porely," Mrs. Harris admitted.

"You stay where you air, ma'am. I'll git the breakfast fur the chillun, an' take the other breakfast in fur Miss Victoria an' Mr. Templeton." She hurried back to the kitchen, and Mrs. Harris went to sleep.

Immediately after breakfast Vickie dashed

off about her own concerns, and the twins went to cut grass while the dew was still on it. When Mandy was taking the other breakfast into the dining-room, Mrs. Templeton came through the play-room.

"What's the matter, Ma? Are you sick?" she asked in an accusing tone.

"No, Victoria, I ain't sick. I had a little giddy spell, and I thought I'd lay still."

"You ought to be more careful what you eat, Ma. If you're going to have another bilious spell, when everything is so upset anyhow, I don't know what I'll do!" Victoria's voice broke. She hurried back into her bedroom, feeling bitterly that there was no place in that house to cry in, no spot where one could be alone, even with misery; that the house and the people in it were choking her to death.

Mrs. Harris sighed and closed her eyes. Things did seem to be upset, though she didn't know just why. Mandy, however, had her suspicions. While she waited on Mr. and Mrs. Templeton at breakfast, narrowly observing their manner toward each other and Victoria's swollen eyes and desperate expression, her suspicions grew stronger.

Instead of going to his office, Mr. Templeton went to the barn and ran out the buggy. Soon he brought out Cleveland, the black horse, with his harness on. Mandy watched from the back window. After he had hitched the horse to the buggy, he came into the kitchen to wash his hands. While he dried them on the roller towel, he said in his most business-like tone:

"I likely won't be back tonight, Mandy. I have to go out to my farm, and I'll hardly get through my business there in time to come home."

Then Mandy was sure. She had been through these times before, and at such a crisis poor Mr. Templeton was always called away on important business. When he had driven out through the alley and up the street past Mrs. Rosen's, Mandy left her dishes and went in to Mrs. Harris. She bent over and whispered low:

"Miz' Harris, I 'spect Miss Victoria's done

found out she's goin' to have another baby! It looks that way. She's gone back to bed."

Mrs. Harris lifted a warning finger. " Sh-h-h! "

" Oh yes'm, I won't say nothin'. I never do."

Mrs. Harris tried to face this possibility, but her mind didn't seem strong enough — she dropped off into another doze.

All that morning Mrs. Templeton lay on her bed alone, the room darkened and a handkerchief soaked in camphor tied round her forehead. The twins had taken Ronald off to watch them cut grass, and Hughie played in the kitchen under Mandy's eye.

Now and then Victoria sat upright on the edge of the bed, beat her hands together softly and looked desperately at the ceiling, then about at those frail, confining walls. If only she could meet the situation with violence, fight it, conquer it! But there was nothing for it but stupid animal patience. She would have to go through all that again, and nobody, not even Hillary, wanted another baby, — poor as they were, and in this overcrowded house. Anyhow, she told herself, she was ashamed to have another baby, when she had a daughter old enough to go to college! She was sick of it all; sick of dragging this chain of life that never let her rest and periodically knotted and overpowered her; made her ill and hideous for months, and then dropped another baby into her arms. She had had babies enough; and there ought to be an end to such apprehensions some time before you were old and ugly.

She wanted to run away, back to Tennessee, and lead a free, gay life, as she had when she was first married. She could do a great deal more with freedom than ever Vickie could. She was still young, and she was still handsome; why must she be for ever shut up in a little cluttered house with children and fresh babies and an old woman and a stupid bound girl and a husband who wasn't very successful? Life hadn't brought her what she expected when she married Hillary Templeton; life hadn't used her right. She had tried to keep up appearances, to dress well with very little to do it on, to keep young for her husband

and children. She had tried, she had tried! Mrs.
Templeton buried her face in the pillow and
smothered the sobs that shook the bed.

Hillary Templeton, on his drive out through
the sage-brush, up into the farming country
that was irrigated from the North Platte, did
not feel altogether cheerful, though he whistled
and sang to himself on the way. He was sorry
Victoria would have to go through another
time. It was awkward just now, too, when he
was so short of money. But he was naturally a
cheerful man, modest in his demands upon
fortune, and easily diverted from unpleasant
thoughts. Before Cleveland had travelled half
the eighteen miles to the farm, his master was
already looking forward to a visit with his
tenants, an old German couple who were fond
of him because he never pushed them in a
hard year — so far, all the years had been hard
— and he sometimes brought them bananas
and such delicacies from town.

Mrs. Heyse would open her best preserves
for him, he knew, and kill a chicken, and

tonight he would have a clean bed in her spare room. She always put a vase of flowers in his room when he stayed overnight with them, and that pleased him very much. He felt like a youth out there, and forgot all the bills he had somehow to meet, and the loans he had made and couldn't collect. The Heyses kept bees and raised turkeys, and had honeysuckle vines running over the front porch. He loved all those things. Mr. Templeton touched Cleveland with the whip, and as they sped along into the grass country, sang softly:

> "Old Jesse was a gem'man,
> Way down in Tennessee."

XIII

Mandy had to manage the house herself that day, and she was not at all sorry. There wasn't a great deal of variety in her life, and she felt very important taking Mrs. Harris's place, giving the children their dinner, and carrying

a plate of milk toast to Mrs. Templeton. She
was worried about Mrs. Harris, however, and
remarked to the children at noon that she
thought somebody ought to " set " with their
grandma. Vickie wasn't home for dinner. She
had her father's office to herself for the day
and was making the most of it, writing a long
letter to Professor Chalmers. Mr. Rosen had
invited her to have dinner with him at the hotel
(he boarded there when his wife was away),
and that was a great honour.

When Mandy said someone ought to be with
the old lady, Bert and Del offered to take
turns. Adelbert went off to rake up the grass
they had been cutting all morning, and Albert
sat down in the play-room. It seemed to him
his grandmother looked pretty sick. He
watched her while Mandy gave her toast-
water with whisky in it, and thought he would
like to make the room look a little nicer. While
Mrs. Harris lay with her eyes closed, he hung
up the caps and coats lying about, and moved
away the big rocking-chair that stood by the
head of Grandma's bed. There ought to be a

table there, he believed, but the small tables in
the house all had something on them. Upstairs,
in the room where he and Adelbert and Ronald
slept, there was a nice clean wooden cracker-
box, on which they sat in the morning to put
on their shoes and stockings. He brought this
down and stood it on end at the head of Grandma's lounge, and put a clean napkin over the
top of it.

She opened her eyes and smiled at him.
" Could you git me a tin of fresh water,
honey? "

He went to the back porch and pumped till
the water ran cold. He gave it to her in a tin
cup as she had asked, but he didn't think that
was the right way. After she dropped back on
the pillow, he fetched a glass tumbler from the
cupboard, filled it, and set it on the table he
had just manufactured. When Grandmother
drew a red cotton handkerchief from under
her pillow and wiped the moisture from her
face, he ran upstairs again and got one of his
Sunday-school handkerchiefs, linen ones, that
Mrs. Rosen had given him and Del for Christ-

mas. Having put this in Grandmother's hand and taken away the crumpled red one, he could think of nothing else to do — except to darken the room a little. The windows had no blinds, but flimsy cretonne curtains tied back, — not really tied, but caught back over nails driven into the sill. He loosened them and let them hang down over the bright afternoon sunlight. Then he sat down on the low sawed-off chair and gazed about, thinking that now it looked quite like a sick-room.

It was hard for a little boy to keep still. "Would you like me to read *Joe's Luck* to you, Gram'ma?" he said presently.

"You might, Bertie."

He got the "boy's book" she had been reading aloud to them, and began where she had left off. Mrs. Harris liked to hear his voice, and she liked to look at him when she opened her eyes from time to time. She did not follow the story. In her mind she was repeating a passage from the second part of *Pilgrim's Progress,* which she had read aloud to the children so many times; the passage where

Christiana and her band come to the arbour on the Hill of Difficulty: *"Then said Mercy, how sweet is rest to them that labour."*

At about four o'clock Adelbert came home, hot and sweaty from raking. He said he had got in the grass and taken it to their cow, and if Bert was reading, he guessed he'd like to listen. He dragged the wooden rocking-chair up close to Grandma's bed and curled up in it.

Grandmother was perfectly happy. She and the twins were about the same age; they had in common all the realest and truest things. The years between them and her, it seemed to Mrs. Harris, were full of trouble and unimportant. The twins and Ronald and Hughie were important. She opened her eyes.

"Where is Hughie?" she asked.

"I guess he's asleep. Mother took him into her bed."

"And Ronald?"

"He's upstairs with Mandy. There ain't nobody in the kitchen now."

"Then you might git me a fresh drink, Del."

"Yes'm, Gram'ma." He tiptoed out to the pump in his brown canvas sneakers.

When Vickie came home at five o'clock, she went to her mother's room, but the door was locked — a thing she couldn't remember ever happening before. She went into the playroom, — old Mrs. Harris was asleep, with one of the twins on guard, and he held up a warning finger. She went into the kitchen. Mandy was making biscuits, and Ronald was helping her to cut them out.

"What's the matter, Mandy? Where is everybody?"

"You know your papa's away, Miss Vickie; an' your mama's got a headache, an' Miz' Harris has had a bad spell. Maybe I'll just fix supper for you an' the boys in the kitchen, so you won't all have to be runnin' through her room."

"Oh, very well," said Vickie bitterly, and she went upstairs. Wasn't it just like them all to go and get sick, when she had now only two weeks to get ready for school, and no trunk and no clothes or anything? Nobody but Mr.

Rosen seemed to take the least interest, "when my whole life hangs by a thread," she told herself fiercely. What were families for, anyway?

After supper Vickie went to her father's office to read; she told Mandy to leave the kitchen door open, and when she got home she would go to bed without disturbing anybody. The twins ran out to play under the electric light with the neighbour boys for a little while, then slipped softly up the back stairs to their room. Mandy came to Mrs. Harris after the house was still.

"Kin I rub your legs fur you, Miz' Harris?"

"Thank you, Mandy. And you might get me a clean nightcap out of the press."

Mandy returned with it.

"Lawsie me! But your legs is cold, ma'am!"

"I expect it's about time, Mandy," murmured the old lady. Mandy knelt on the floor and set to work with a will. It brought the sweat out on her, and at last she sat up and wiped her face with the back of her hand.

"I can't seem to git no heat into 'em, Miz'

Harris. I got a hot flat-iron on the stove; I'll
wrap it in a piece of old blanket and put it to
your feet. Why didn't you have the boys tell
me you was cold, pore soul?"

Mrs. Harris did not answer. She thought it
was probably a cold that neither Mandy nor
the flat-iron could do much with. She hadn't
nursed so many people back in Tennessee
without coming to know certain signs.

After Mandy was gone, she fell to thinking
of her blessings. Every night for years, when
she said her prayers, she had prayed that she
might never have a long sickness or be a burden. She dreaded the heart-ache and humilia-
tion of being helpless on the hands of people
who would be impatient under such a care.
And now she felt certain that she was going
to die tonight, without troubling anybody.

She was glad Mrs. Rosen was in Chicago.
Had she been at home, she would certainly
have come in, would have seen that her old
neighbour was very sick, and bustled about.
Her quick eye would have found out all Grandmother's little secrets: how hard her bed was,

that she had no proper place to wash, and kept her comb in her pocket; that her nightgowns were patched and darned. Mrs. Rosen would have been indignant, and that would have made Victoria cross. She didn't have to see Mrs. Rosen again to know that Mrs. Rosen thought highly of her and admired her — yes, admired her. Those funny little pats and arch pleasantries had meant a great deal to Mrs. Harris.

It was a blessing that Mr. Templeton was away, too. Appearances had to be kept up when there was a man in the house; and he might have taken it into his head to send for the doctor, and stir everybody up. Now everything would be so peaceful. "*The Lord is my shepherd*," she whispered gratefully. "Yes, Lord, I always spoiled Victoria. She was so much the prettiest. But nobody won't ever be the worse for it: Mr. Templeton will always humour her, and the children love her more than most. They'll always be good to her; she has that way with her."

Grandma fell to remembering the old place at home: what a dashing, high-spirited girl

Victoria was, and how proud she had always been of her; how she used to hear her laughing and teasing out in the lilac arbour when Hillary Templeton was courting her. Toward morning all these pleasant reflections faded out. Mrs. Harris felt that she and her bed were softly sinking, through the darkness to a deeper darkness.

Old Mrs. Harris did not really die that night, but she believed she did. Mandy found her unconscious in the morning. Then there was a great stir and bustle; Victoria, and even Vickie, were startled out of their intense self-absorption. Mrs. Harris was hastily carried out of the play-room and laid in Victoria's bed, put into one of Victoria's best nightgowns. Mr. Templeton was sent for, and the doctor was sent for. The inquisitive Mrs. Jackson from next door got into the house at last, — installed herself as nurse, and no one had the courage to say her nay. But Grandmother was out of it all, never knew that she was the object of so much attention and excitement. She died a little while after Mr. Templeton got home.

Thus Mrs. Harris slipped out of the Templetons' story; but Victoria and Vickie had still to go on, to follow the long road that leads through things unguessed at and unforeseeable. When they are old, they will come closer and closer to Grandma Harris. They will think a great deal about her, and remember things they never noticed; and their lot will be more or less like hers. They will regret that they heeded her so little; but they, too, will look into the eager, unseeing eyes of young people and feel themselves alone. They will say to themselves: "I was heartless, because I was young and strong and wanted things so much. But now I know."

New Brunswick, 1931

TWO FRIENDS

TWO FRIENDS

I

Even in early youth, when the mind is so eager for the new and untried, while it is still a stranger to faltering and fear, we yet like to think that there are certain unalterable realities, somewhere at the bottom of things. These anchors may be ideas; but more often they are merely pictures, vivid memories, which in some unaccountable and very personal way give us courage. The sea-gulls, that seem so much creatures of the free wind and waves, that are as homeless as the sea (able to rest upon the tides and ride the storm, needing nothing but water and sky), at certain seasons even they go back to something they have known before; to remote islands and lonely ledges that are their breeding-grounds. The restlessness of youth has such retreats, even though it may be ashamed of them.

Long ago, before the invention of the motor-car (which has made more changes in the world than the War, which indeed produced the particular kind of war that happened just a hundred years after Waterloo), in a little wooden town in a shallow Kansas river valley, there lived two friends. They were " business men," the two most prosperous and influential men in our community, the two men whose affairs took them out into the world to big cities, who had " connections " in St. Joseph and Chicago. In my childhood they represented to me success and power.

R. E. Dillon was of Irish extraction, one of the dark Irish, with glistening jet-black hair and moustache, and thick eyebrows. His skin was very white, bluish on his shaven cheeks and chin. Shaving must have been a difficult process for him, because there were no smooth expanses for the razor to glide over. The bony structure of his face was prominent and unusual; high

cheek-bones, a bold Roman nose, a chin cut by
deep lines, with a hard dimple at the tip, a jut-
ting ridge over his eyes where his curly black
eyebrows grew and met. It was a face in many
planes, as if the carver had whittled and mod-
elled and indented to see how far he could go.
Yet on meeting him what you saw was an imperious head on a rather small, wiry man, a head
held conspicuously and proudly erect, with a
carriage unmistakably arrogant and con-
sciously superior. Dillon had a musical, vibrat-
ing voice, and the changeable grey eye that is
peculiarly Irish. His full name, which he never
used, was Robert Emmet Dillon, so there must
have been a certain feeling somewhere back in
his family.

He was the principal banker in our town, and
proprietor of the large general store next the
bank; he owned farms up in the grass country, and a fine ranch in the green timbered valley of the Caw. He was, according to our stand-
ards, a rich man.

His friend, J. H. Trueman, was what we
called a big cattleman. Trueman was from

Buffalo; his family were old residents there, and he had come West as a young man because he was restless and unconventional in his tastes. He was fully ten years older than Dillon, — in his early fifties, when I knew him; large, heavy, very slow in his movements, not given to exercise. His countenance was as unmistakably American as Dillon's was not, — but American of that period, not of this. He did not belong to the time of efficiency and advertising and progressive methods. For any form of pushing or boosting he had a cold, unqualified contempt. All this was in his face, — heavy, immobile, rather melancholy, not remarkable in any particular. But the moment one looked at him one felt solidity, an entire absence of anything mean or small, easy carelessness, courage, a high sense of honour.

These two men had been friends for ten years before I knew them, and I knew them from the time I was ten until I was thirteen. I saw them as often as I could, because they led more varied lives than the other men in our town; one could look up to them. Dillon, I believe, was the more intelligent. Trueman had, perhaps, a better tradition, more background.

Dillon's bank and general store stood at the corner of Main Street and a cross-street, and on this cross-street, two short blocks away, my family lived. On my way to and from school, and going on the countless errands that I was sent upon day and night, I always passed Dillon's store. Its long, red brick wall, with no windows except high overhead, ran possibly a hundred feet along the sidewalk of the cross-street. The front door and show windows were on Main Street, and the bank was next door. The board sidewalk along that red brick wall was wider than any other piece of walk in town, smoother, better laid, kept in perfect repair; very good to walk on in a community where most things were flimsy. I liked the store and the brick wall and the sidewalk because they were solid and well built, and possibly I admired Dillon and Trueman for much the same reason. They were secure and established. So many of our citizens were nervous little hopper men, trying to get on. Dillon and

Trueman had got on; they stood with easy
assurance on a deck that was their own.

In the daytime one did not often see them
together — each went about his own affairs.
But every evening they were both to be found
at Dillon's store. The bank, of course, was
locked and dark before the sun went down, but
the store was always open until ten o'clock;
the clerks put in a long day. So did Dillon. He
and his store were one. He never acted as sales-
man, and he kept a cashier in the wire-screened
office at the back end of the store; but he was
there to be called on. The thrifty Swedes to the
north, who were his best customers, usually
came to town and did their shopping after dark
— they didn't squander daylight hours in
farming season. In these evening visits with his
customers, and on his drives in his buckboard
among the farms, Dillon learned all he needed
to know about how much money it was safe to
advance a farmer who wanted to feed cattle, or
to buy a steam thrasher or build a new barn.

Every evening in winter, when I went to
the post-office after supper, I passed through

Dillon's store instead of going round it, — for the warmth and cheerfulness, and to catch sight of Mr. Dillon and Mr. Trueman playing checkers in the office behind the wire screening; both seated on high accountant's stools, with the checker-board on the cashier's desk before them. I knew all Dillon's clerks, and if they were not busy, I often lingered about to talk to them; sat on one of the grocery counters and watched the checker-players from a distance. I remember Mr. Dillon's hand used to linger in the air above the board before he made a move; a well-kept hand, white, marked with blue veins and streaks of strong black hair. Trueman's hands rested on his knees under the desk while he considered; he took a checker, set it down, then dropped his hand on his knee again. He seldom made an unnecessary movement with his hands or feet. Each of the men wore a ring on his little finger. Mr. Dillon's was a large diamond solitaire set in a gold claw, Trueman's the head of a Roman soldier cut in onyx and set in pale twisted gold; it had been his father's, I believe.

TWO FRIENDS

Exactly at ten o'clock the store closed. Mr. Dillon went home to his wife and family, to his roomy, comfortable house with a garden and orchard and big stables. Mr. Trueman, who had long been a widower, went to his office to begin the day over. He led a double life, and until one or two o'clock in the morning entertained the poker-players of our town. After everything was shut for the night, a queer crowd drifted into Trueman's back office. The company was seldom the same on two successive evenings, but there were three tireless poker-players who always came: the billiard-hall proprietor, with green-gold moustache and eyebrows, and big white teeth; the horse-trader, who smelled of horses; the dandified cashier of the bank that rivalled Dillon's. The gamblers met in Trueman's place because a game that went on there was respectable, was a social game, no matter how much money changed hands. If the horse-trader or the crooked money-lender got over-heated and broke loose a little, a look or a remark from Mr. Trueman would freeze them up. And his remark was always the same:

"Careful of the language around here."

It was never "your" language, but "the" language, — though he certainly intended no pleasantry. Trueman himself was not a lucky poker man; he was never ahead of the game on the whole. He played because he liked it, and he was willing to pay for his amusement. In general he was large and indifferent about money matters, — always carried a few hundred-dollar bills in his inside coat-pocket, and left his coat hanging anywhere, — in his office, in the bank, in the barber shop, in the cattle-sheds behind the freight yard.

Now, R. E. Dillon detested gambling, often dropped a contemptuous word about "poker bugs" before the horse-trader and the billiard-hall man and the cashier of the other bank. But he never made remarks of that sort in Trueman's presence. He was a man who voiced his prejudices fearlessly and cuttingly, but on this and other matters he held his peace before Trueman. His regard for him must have been very strong.

During the winter, usually in March, the two friends always took a trip together, to Kansas City and St. Joseph. When they got ready, they packed their bags and stepped aboard a fast Santa Fé train and went; the Limited was often signalled to stop for them. Their excursions made some of the rest of us feel less shut away and small-townish, just as their fur overcoats and silk shirts did. They were the only men in Singleton who wore silk shirts. The other business men wore white shirts with detachable collars, high and stiff or low and sprawling, which were changed much oftener than the shirts. Neither of my heroes was afraid of laundry bills. They did not wear waistcoats, but went about in their shirt-sleeves in hot weather; their suspenders were chosen with as much care as their neckties and handkerchiefs. Once when a bee stung my hand in the store (a few of them had got into the brown-sugar barrel), Mr. Dillon himself moistened the sting, put baking soda on it, and bound my hand up with his pocket handkerchief. It was of the smoothest linen, and in one corner was a violet square bearing his initials, R. E. D., in white. There were never any handkerchiefs like that in my family. I cherished it until it was laundered, and I returned it with regret.

It was in the spring and summer that one saw Mr. Dillon and Mr. Trueman at their best. Spring began early with us, — often the first week of April was hot. Every evening when he came back to the store after supper, Dillon had one of his clerks bring two arm-chairs out to the wide sidewalk that ran beside the red brick wall, — office chairs of the old-fashioned sort, with a low round back which formed a half-circle to enclose the sitter, and spreading legs, the front ones slightly higher. In those chairs the two friends would spend the evening. Dillon would sit down and light a good cigar. In a few moments Mr. Trueman would come across from Main Street, walking slowly, spaciously, as if he were used to a great deal of room. As he approached, Mr. Dillon would call out to him:

"Good evening, J. H. Fine weather."

J. H. would take his place in the empty chair.

"Spring in the air," he might remark, if it were April. Then he would relight a dead cigar which was always in his hand, — seemed to belong there, like a thumb or finger.

"I drove up north today to see what the Swedes are doing," Mr. Dillon might begin. "They're the boys to get the early worm. They never let the ground go to sleep. Whatever moisture there is, they get the benefit of it."

"The Swedes are good farmers. I don't sympathize with the way they work their women."

"The women like it, J. H. It's the old-country way; they're accustomed to it, and they like it."

"Maybe. I don't like it," Trueman would reply with something like a grunt.

They talked very much like this all evening; or, rather, Mr. Dillon talked, and Mr. Trueman made an occasional observation. No one could tell just how much Mr. Trueman knew about anything, because he was so consistently silent. Not from diffidence, but from superiority; from a contempt for chatter, and a liking for silence, a taste for it. After they had exchanged a few remarks, he and Dillon often sat in an easy quiet for a long time, watching the passers-by, watching the wagons on the road, watching the stars. Sometimes, very rarely, Mr. Trueman told a long story, and it was sure to be an interesting and unusual one.

But on the whole it was Mr. Dillon who did the talking; he had a wide-awake voice with much variety in it. Trueman's was thick and low, — his speech was rather indistinct and never changed in pitch or tempo. Even when he swore wickedly at the hands who were loading his cattle into freight cars, it was a mutter, a low, even growl. There was a curious attitude in men of his class and time, that of being rather above speech, as they were above any kind of fussiness or eagerness. But I knew he liked to hear Mr. Dillon talk, — anyone did. Dillon had such a crisp, clear enunciation, and he could say things so neatly. People would take a reprimand from him they wouldn't have taken from anyone else, because he put it so well. His voice was never warm or soft — it had a cool, sparkling quality; but it could be very humorous, very kind and considerate, very teasing and stimulating. Every sentence he uttered was alive, never languid, perfunctory, slovenly, unaccented. When he made a remark, it not only meant something, but sounded like something, — sounded like the thing he meant.

When Mr. Dillon was closeted with a depositor in his private room in the bank, and you could not hear his words through the closed door, his voice told you exactly the degree of esteem in which he held that customer. It was interested, encouraging, deliberative, humorous, satisfied, admiring, cold, critical, haughty, contemptuous, according to the deserts and pretensions of his listener. And one could tell when the person closeted with him was a woman; a farmer's wife, or a woman who was trying to run a little business, or a country girl hunting a situation. There was a difference; something peculiarly kind and encouraging. But if it were a foolish, extravagant woman, or a girl he didn't approve of, oh, then one knew it well enough! The tone was courteous, but cold; relentless as the multiplication table.

All these possibilities of voice made his evening talk in the spring dusk very interesting; interesting for Trueman and for me. I found many pretexts for lingering near them, and they never seemed to mind my hanging about. I was very quiet. I often sat on the edge of the sidewalk with my feet hanging down and played jacks by the hour when there was moonlight. On dark nights I sometimes perched on top of one of the big goods-boxes — we called them "store boxes," — there were usually several of these standing empty on the sidewalk against the red brick wall.

I liked to listen to those two because theirs was the only "conversation" one could hear about the streets. The older men talked of nothing but politics and their business, and the very young men's talk was entirely what they called "josh"; very personal, supposed to be funny, and really not funny at all. It was scarcely speech, but noises, snorts, giggles, yawns, sneezes, with a few abbreviated words and slang expressions which stood for a hundred things. The original Indians of the Kansas plains had more to do with articulate speech than had our promising young men.

To be sure my two aristocrats sometimes discussed politics, and joked each other about the policies and pretentions of their respective parties. Mr. Dillon, of course, was a Democrat, — it was in the very frosty sparkle of his speech, — and Mr. Trueman was a Republican; his rear, as he walked about the town, looked a little like the walking elephant labelled " G. O. P." in *Puck*. But each man seemed to enjoy hearing his party ridiculed, took it as a compliment.

In the spring their talk was usually about weather and planting and pasture and cattle. Mr. Dillon went about the country in his light buckboard a great deal at that season, and he knew what every farmer was doing and what his chances were, just how much he was falling behind or getting ahead.

" I happened to drive by Oscar Ericson's place today, and I saw as nice a lot of calves as you could find anywhere," he would begin, and Ericson's history and his family would be pretty thoroughly discussed before they changed the subject.

Or he might come out with something sharp: "By the way, J. H., I saw an amusing sight today. I turned in at Sandy Bright's place to get water for my horse, and he had a photographer out there taking pictures of his house and barn. It would be more to the point if he had a picture taken of the mortgages he's put on that farm."

Trueman would give a short, mirthless response, more like a cough than a laugh.

Those April nights, when the darkness itself tasted dusty (or, by the special mercy of God, cool and damp), when the smell of burning grass was in the air, and a sudden breeze brought the scent of wild plum blossoms, — those evenings were only a restless preparation for the summer nights, — nights of full liberty and perfect idleness. Then there was no school, and one's family never bothered about where one was. My parents were young and full of

life, glad to have the children out of the way.
All day long there had been the excitement that
intense heat produces in some people, — a mild
drunkenness made of sharp contrasts; thirst
and cold water, the blazing stretch of Main
Street and the cool of the brick stores when
one dived into them. By nightfall one was
ready to be quiet. My two friends were
always in their best form on those moonlit
summer nights, and their talk covered a wide
range.

I suppose there were moonless nights, and
dark ones with but a silver shaving and pale
stars in the sky, just as in the spring. But I remember them all as flooded by the rich indo-
lence of a full moon, or a half-moon set in uncertain blue. Then Trueman and Dillon would
sit with their coats off and have a supply of
fresh handkerchiefs to mop their faces; they
were more largely and positively themselves.
One could distinguish their features, the stripes
on their shirts, the flash of Mr. Dillon's diamond; but their shadows made two dark
masses on the white sidewalk. The brick

wall behind them, faded almost pink by the
burning of successive summers, took on a carnelian hue at night. Across the street, which
was merely a dusty road, lay an open space,
with a few stunted box-elder trees, where the
farmers left their wagons and teams when they
came to town. Beyond this space stood a row
of frail wooden buildings, due to be pulled
down any day; tilted, crazy, with outside stairs
going up to rickety second-storey porches that
sagged in the middle. They had once been
white, but were now grey, with faded blue
doors along the wavy upper porches. These
abandoned buildings, an eyesore by day,
melted together into a curious pile in the moonlight, became an immaterial structure of velvet-
white and glossy blackness, with here and
there a faint smear of blue door, or a tilted
patch of sage-green that had once been a
shutter.

The road, just in front of the sidewalk where
I sat and played jacks, would be ankle-deep in
dust, and seemed to drink up the moonlight
like folds of velvet. It drank up sound, too;

muffled the wagon-wheels and hoof-beats; lay
soft and meek like the last residuum of mate-
rial things, — the soft bottom resting-place.
Nothing in the world, not snow mountains or
blue seas, is so beautiful in moonlight as the
soft, dry summer roads in a farming country,
roads where the white dust falls back from the
slow wagon-wheel.

Wonderful things do happen even in the
dullest places — in the cornfields and the
wheat-fields. Sitting there on the edge of the
sidewalk one summer night, my feet hanging in
the warm dust, I saw an occultation of Venus.
Only the three of us were there. It was a hot
night, and the clerks had closed the store and
gone home. Mr. Dillon and Mr. Trueman
waited on a little while to watch. It was a very
blue night, breathless and clear, not the small-
est cloud from horizon to horizon. Everything
up there overhead seemed as usual, it was the
familiar face of a summer-night sky. But presently we saw one bright star moving. Mr. Dillon called to me; told me to watch what was

going to happen, as I might never chance to see it again in my lifetime.

That big star certainly got nearer and nearer the moon, — very rapidly, too, until there was not the width of your hand between them — now the width of two fingers — then it passed directly into the moon at about the middle of its girth; absolutely disappeared. The star we had been watching was gone. We waited, I do not know how long, but it seemed to me about fifteen minutes. Then we saw a bright wart on the other edge of the moon, but for a second only, — the machinery up there worked fast. While the two men were exclaiming and telling me to look, the planet swung clear of the golden disk, a rift of blue came between them and widened very fast. The planet did not seem to move, but that inky blue space between it and the moon seemed to spread. The thing was over.

My friends stayed on long past their usual time and talked about eclipses and such matters.

"Let me see," Mr. Trueman remarked

slowly, "they reckon the moon's about two hundred and fifty thousand miles away from us. I wonder how far that star is."

"I don't know, J. H., and I really don't much care. When we can get the tramps off the railroad, and manage to run this town with one fancy house instead of two, and have a Federal Government that is as honest as a good banking business, then it will be plenty of time to turn our attention to the stars."

Mr. Trueman chuckled and took his cigar from between his teeth. "Maybe the stars will throw some light on all that, if we get the run of them," he said humorously. Then he added: "Mustn't be a reformer, R. E. Nothing in it. That's the only time you ever get off on the wrong foot. Life is what it always has been, always will be. No use to make a fuss." He got up, said: "Good-night, R. E.," said good-night to me, too, because this had been an unusual occasion, and went down the sidewalk with his wide, sailor-like tread, as if he were walking the deck of his own ship.

When Dillon and Trueman went to St. Jo-

seph, or, as we called it, St. Joe, they stopped
at the same hotel, but their diversions were very
dissimilar. Mr. Dillon was a family man and
a good Catholic; he behaved in St. Joe very
much as if he were at home. His sister was
Mother Superior of a convent there, and he
went to see her often. The nuns made much of
him, and he enjoyed their admiration and all
the ceremony with which they entertained him.
When his two daughters were going to the
convent school, he used to give theatre parties
for them, inviting all their friends.

Mr. Trueman's way of amusing himself
must have tried his friend's patience — Dillon liked to regulate other people's affairs if
they needed it. Mr. Trueman had a lot of poker-
playing friends among the commission men in
St. Joe, and he sometimes dropped a good deal
of money. He was supposed to have rather
questionable women friends there, too. The
grasshopper men of our town used to say that
Trueman was financial adviser to a woman
who ran a celebrated sporting house. Mary
Trent, her name was. She must have been a

very unusual woman; she had credit with all the banks, and never got into any sort of trouble. She had formerly been head mistress of a girls' finishing school and knew how to manage young women. It was probably a fact that Trueman knew her and found her interesting, as did many another sound business man of that time. Mr. Dillon must have shut his ears to these rumours, — a measure of the great value he put on Trueman's companionship.

Though they did not see much of each other on these trips, they immensely enjoyed taking them together. They often dined together at the end of the day, and afterwards went to the theatre. They both loved the theatre; not this play or that actor, but the theatre, — whether they saw *Hamlet* or *Pinafore*. It was an age of good acting, and the drama held a more dignified position in the world than it holds today.

After Dillon and Trueman had come home from the city, they used sometimes to talk over the plays they had seen, recalling the great scenes and fine effects. Occasionally an item in the Kansas City *Star* would turn their talk to the stage.

"J. H., I see by the paper that Edwin Booth is very sick," Mr. Dillon announced one evening as Trueman came up to take the empty chair.

"Yes, I noticed." Trueman sat down and lit his dead cigar. "He's not a young man any more." A long pause. Dillon always seemed to know when the pause would be followed by a remark, and waited for it. "The first time I saw Edwin Booth was in Buffalo. It was in *Richard the Second,* and it made a great impression on me at the time." Another pause. "I don't know that I'd care to see him in that play again. I like tragedy, but that play's a little too tragic. Something very black about it. I think I prefer *Hamlet*."

They had seen Mary Anderson in St. Louis once, and talked of it for years afterwards. Mr. Dillon was very proud of her because she was a Catholic girl, and called her "our Mary." It was curious that a third person, who had never seen these actors or read the plays, could get so much of the essence of both from the comments of two business men who used none of the language in which such things are usually discussed, who merely reminded each other of moments here and there in the action. But they saw the play over again as they talked of it, and perhaps whatever is seen by the narrator as he speaks is sensed by the listener, quite irrespective of words. This transference of experience went further: in some way the lives of those two men came across to me as they talked, the strong, bracing reality of successful, large-minded men who had made their way in the world when business was still a personal adventure.

II

Mr. Dillon went to Chicago once a year to buy goods for his store. Trueman would usually accompany him as far as St. Joe, but no farther. He dismissed Chicago as "too big." He didn't like to be one of the crowd, didn't feel at home in a city where he wasn't recognized as J. H. Trueman.

It was one of these trips to Chicago that brought about the end — for me and for them; a stupid, senseless, commonplace end.

Being a Democrat, already somewhat "tainted" by the free-silver agitation, one spring Dillon delayed his visit to Chicago in order to be there for the Democratic Convention — it was the Convention that first nominated Bryan.

On the night after his return from Chicago, Mr. Dillon was seated in his chair on the sidewalk, surrounded by a group of men who wanted to hear all about the nomination of a man from a neighbour State. Mr. Trueman came across the street in his leisurely way, greeted Dillon, and asked him how he had found Chicago, — whether he had had a good trip.

Mr. Dillon must have been annoyed because Trueman didn't mention the Convention. He threw back his head rather haughtily. "Well,

J. H., since I saw you last, we've found a great leader in this country, and a great orator." There was a frosty sparkle in his voice that presupposed opposition, — like the feint of a boxer getting ready.

" Great windbag! " muttered Trueman. He sat down in his chair, but I noticed that he did not settle himself and cross his legs as usual.

Mr. Dillon gave an artificial laugh. " It's nothing against a man to be a fine orator. All the great leaders have been eloquent. This Convention was a memorable occasion; it gave the Democratic party a rebirth."

" Gave it a black eye, and a blind spot, I'd say! " commented Trueman. He didn't raise his voice, but he spoke with more heat than I had ever heard from him. After a moment he added: " I guess Grover Cleveland must be a sick man; must feel like he'd taken a lot of trouble for nothing."

Mr. Dillon ignored these thrusts and went on telling the group around him about the Convention, but there was a special nimbleness and exactness in his tongue, a chill politeness in his voice that meant anger. Presently he turned again to Mr. Trueman, as if he could now trust himself:

"It was one of the great speeches of history, J. H.; our grandchildren will have to study it in school, as we did Patrick Henry's."

"Glad I haven't got any grandchildren, if they'd be brought up on that sort of tall talk," said Mr. Trueman. "Sounds like a schoolboy had written it. Absolutely nothing back of it but an unsound theory."

Mr. Dillon's laugh made me shiver; it was like a thin glitter of danger. He arched his curly eyebrows provokingly.

"We'll have four years of currency reform, anyhow. By the end of that time, you old dyed-in-the-wool Republicans will be thinking differently. The under dog is going to have a chance."

Mr. Trueman shifted in his chair. "That's no way for a banker to talk." He spoke very low. "The Democrats will have a long time to be sorry they ever turned Pops. No use talking to you while your Irish is up. I'll wait till you cool off." He rose and walked away, less deliberately than usual, and Mr. Dillon, watching his retreating figure, laughed haughtily and disagreeably. He asked the grain-elevator man to take the vacated chair. The group about him grew, and he sat expounding the reforms proposed by the Democratic candidate until a late hour.

For the first time in my life I listened with breathless interest to a political discussion. Whoever Mr. Dillon failed to convince, he convinced me. I grasped it at once: that gold had been responsible for most of the miseries and inequalities of the world; that it had always been the club the rich and cunning held over the poor; and that " the free and unlimited coinage of silver " would remedy all this. Dillon declared that young Mr. Bryan had looked like the patriots of old when he faced and challenged high finance with: " You shall not press this crown of thorns upon the brow of labour; you shall not crucify mankind upon a cross of gold." I thought that magnificent; I thought the cornfields would show them a thing or two, back there!

R. E. Dillon had never taken an aggressive part in politics. But from that night on, the Democratic candidate and the free-silver plank were the subject of his talks with his customers and depositors. He drove about the country convincing the farmers, went to the neighbouring towns to use his influence with the merchants, organized the Bryan Club and the Bryan Ladies' Quartette in our county, contributed largely to the campaign fund. This was all a new line of conduct for Mr. Dillon, and it sat unsteadily on him. Even his voice became unnatural; there was a sting of comeback in it. His new character made him more like other people and took away from his special personal quality. I wonder whether it was not Trueman, more than Bryan, who put such an edge on him.

While all these things were going on, Trueman kept to his own office. He came to Dillon's bank on business, but he did not " come back to the sidewalk," as I put it to myself. He waited and said nothing, but he looked grim. After a month or so, when he saw that this thing was not going to blow over, when he heard how Dillon had been talking to representative men all over the county, and saw the figure he had put down for the campaign fund, then Trueman remarked to some of his friends that a banker had no business to commit himself to a scatter-brained financial policy which would destroy credit.

The next morning Mr. Trueman went to the bank across the street, the rival of Dillon's, and wrote a cheque on Dillon's bank "for the amount of my balance." He wasn't the sort of man who would ever know what his balance was, he merely kept it big enough to cover emergencies. That afternoon the Merchants' National took the check over to Dillon on its collecting rounds, and by night the word was all over town that Trueman had changed his bank. After this there would be no going back, people said. To change your bank was one of the most final things you could do. The little, unsuccessful men were pleased, as they always are at the destruction of anything strong and fine.

All through the summer and the autumn of that campaign Mr. Dillon was away a great deal. When he was at home, he took his evening airing on the sidewalk, and there was always a group of men about him, talking of the coming election; that was the most exciting presidential campaign people could remember. I often passed this group on my way to the post-office, but there was no temptation to linger now. Mr. Dillon seemed like another man, and my zeal to free humanity from the cross of gold had cooled. Mr. Trueman I seldom saw. When he passed me on the street, he nodded kindly.

The election and Bryan's defeat did nothing to soften Dillon. He had been sure of a Democratic victory. I believe he felt almost as if Trueman were responsible for the triumph of Hanna and McKinley. At least he knew that Trueman was exceedingly well satisfied, and that was bitter to him. He seemed to me sarcastic and sharp all the time now.

I don't believe self-interest would ever have made a breach between Dillon and Trueman. Neither would have taken advantage of the other. If a combination of circumstances had made it necessary that one or the other should take a loss in money or prestige, I think Trueman would have pocketed the loss. That was his way. It was his code, moreover. A gentleman pocketed his gains mechanically, in the day's routine; but he pocketed losses punctiliously, with a sharp, if bitter, relish. I believe now, as I believed then, that this was a quarrel of " principle." Trueman looked down on anyone who could take the reasoning of the Populist party seriously. He was a perfectly direct man, and he showed his contempt. That was enough. It lost me my special pleasure of summer nights: the old stories of the early West that sometimes came to the surface; the minute biographies of the farming people; the clear, detailed, illuminating accounts of all that went on in the great crop-growing, cattle-feeding world; and the silence, — the strong, rich, outflowing silence between two friends, that was as full and satisfying as the moonlight. I was never to know its like again.

After that rupture nothing went well with

either of my two great men. Things were out of true, the equilibrium was gone. Formerly, when they used to sit in their old places on the sidewalk, two black figures with patches of shadow below, they seemed like two bodies held steady by some law of balance, an unconscious relation like that between the earth and the moon. It was this mathematical harmony which gave a third person pleasure.

Before the next presidential campaign came round, Mr. Dillon died (a young man still) very suddenly, of pneumonia. We didn't know that he was seriously ill until one of his clerks came running to our house to tell us he was dead. The same clerk, half out of his wits — it looked like the end of the world to him — ran on to tell Mr. Trueman.

Mr. Trueman thanked him. He called his confidential man, and told him to order flowers from Kansas City. Then he went to his house, informed his housekeeper that he was going away on business, and packed his bag. That same night he boarded the Santa Fé Limited and didn't stop until he was in San Francisco.

He was gone all spring. His confidential clerk wrote him letters every week about the business and the new calves, and got telegrams in reply. Trueman never wrote letters.

When Mr. Trueman at last came home, he stayed only a few months. He sold out everything he owned to a stranger from Kansas City; his feeding ranch, his barns and sheds, his house and town lots. It was a terrible blow to me; now only the common, everyday people would be left. I used to walk mournfully up and down before his office while all these deeds were being signed, — there were usually lawyers and notaries inside. But once, when he happened to be alone, he called me in, asked me how old I was now, and how far along I had got in school. His face and voice were more than kind, but he seemed absent-minded, as if he were trying to recall something. Presently he took from his watch-chain a red seal I had always admired, reached for my hand, and dropped the piece of carnelian into my palm.

" For a keepsake," he said evasively.

When the transfer of his property was completed, Mr. Trueman left us for good. He spent the rest of his life among the golden hills of San Francisco. He moved into the Saint Francis Hotel when it was first built, and had an office in a high building at the top of what is now Powell Street. There he read his letters in the morning and played poker at night. I've heard a man whose offices were next his tell how Trueman used to sit tilted back in his desk chair, a half-consumed cigar in his mouth, morning after morning, apparently doing nothing, watching the Bay and the ferry-boats, across a line of wind-racked eucalyptus trees. He died at the Saint Francis about nine years after he left our part of the world.

The breaking-up of that friendship between two men who scarcely noticed my existence was a real loss to me, and has ever since been a regret. More than once, in Southern countries where there is a smell of dust and dryness in the air and the nights are intense, I have come upon a stretch of dusty white road drinking up the moonlight beside a blind wall, and have felt a sudden sadness. Perhaps it was not until the next morning that I knew why, — and then only because I had dreamed of Mr. Dillon or Mr. Trueman in my sleep. When that old scar is occasionally touched by chance, it rouses the old uneasiness; the feeling of something broken that could so easily have been mended; of something delightful that was senselessly wasted, of a truth that was accidentally distorted — one of the truths we want to keep.

Pasadena, 1931

WILLA CATHER (1873–1947) was born near Winchester, Virginia. When she was ten, her family moved from the peace of Virginia to the wild prairies of Nebraska. She was graduated from the University of Nebraska at twenty-one, and did newspaper work and teaching in Pittsburgh, Pennsylvania, for the next few years. She published a book of verse, *April Twilights,* in 1903, and a book of short stories, *The Troll Garden,* in 1905. They were followed, over the years, by twelve novels, including *Death Comes for the Archbishop, A Lost Lady* and *Shadows on the Rock;* four volumes of short stories, and two volumes of essays. Willa Cather was awarded the Pulitzer Prize for fiction in 1923.

VINTAGE WOMEN'S STUDIES

VINTAGE WORKS OF SCIENCE AND PSYCHOLOGY

VINTAGE FICTION, POETRY, AND PLAYS

V-814   **ABE, KOBO** / The Woman in the Dunes
V-2014   **AUDEN, W. H.** / Collected Longer Poems
V-2015   **AUDEN, W. H.** / Collected Shorter Poems 1927-1957
V-102   **AUDEN, W. H.** / Selected Poetry of W. H. Auden
V-601   **AUDEN, W. H. AND PAUL B. TAYLOR (trans.)** / The Elder Edda
V-20   **BABIN, MARIA-THERESA AND STAN STEINER (eds.)** / Borinquen: An Anthology of Puerto-Rican Literature
V-271   **BEDIER, JOSEPH** / Tristan and Iseult
V-523   **BELLAMY, JOE DAVID (ed.)** / Superfiction or The American Story Transformed: An Anthology
V-72   **BERNIKOW, LOUISE (ed.)** / The World Split Open: Four Centuries of Women Poets in England and America 1552-1950
V-321   **BOLT, ROBERT** / A Man for All Seasons
V-21   **BOWEN, ELIZABETH** / The Death of the Heart
V-294   **BRADBURY, RAY** / The Vintage Bradbury
V-670   **BRECHT, BERTOLT (ed. by Ralph Manheim and John Willett)** / Collected Plays, Vol. 1
V-759   **BRECHT, BERTOLT (ed. by Ralph Manheim and John Willett)** / Collected Plays, Vol. 5
V-216   **BRECHT, BERTOLT (ed. by Ralph Manheim and John Willett)** / Collected Plays, Vol. 7
V-819   **BRECHT, BERTOLT (ed. by Ralph Manheim and John Willett)** / Collected Plays, Vol. 9
V-841   **BYNNER, WITTER AND KIANG KANG-HU (eds.)** / The Jade Mountain: A Chinese Anthology
V-207   **CAMUS, ALBERT** / Caligula & Three Other Plays
V-281   **CAMUS, ALBERT** / Exile and the Kingdom
V-223   **CAMUS, ALBERT** / The Fall
V-865   **CAMUS, ALBERT** / A Happy Death: A Novel
V-626   **CAMUS, ALBERT** / Lyrical and Critical Essays
V-75   **CAMUS, ALBERT** / The Myth of Sisyphus and Other Essays
V-258   **CAMUS, ALBERT** / The Plague
V-245   **CAMUS, ALBERT** / The Possessed
V-30   **CAMUS, ALBERT** / The Rebel
V-2   **CAMUS, ALBERT** / The Stranger
V-28   **CATHER, WILLA** / Five Stories
V-705   **CATHER, WILLA** / A Lost Lady
V-200   **CATHER, WILLA** / My Mortal Enemy
V-179   **CATHER, WILLA** / Obscure Destinies
V-252   **CATHER, WILLA** / One of Ours
V-913   **CATHER, WILLA** / The Professor's House
V-434   **CATHER, WILLA** / Sapphira and the Slave Girl
V-680   **CATHER, WILLA** / Shadows on the Rock
V-684   **CATHER, WILLA** / Youth and the Bright Medusa
V-140   **CERF, BENNETT (ed.)** / Famous Ghost Stories
V-203   **CERF, BENNETT (ed.)** / Four Contemporary American Plays
V-127   **CERF, BENNETT (ed.)** / Great Modern Short Stories
V-326   **CERF, CHRISTOPHER (ed.)** / The Vintage Anthology of Science Fantasy

VINTAGE POLITICAL SCIENCE AND SOCIAL CRITICISM